Office of Scientific Operations - Release #1

Office of Scientific Operations, Volume 1

K McConnell

Published by K McConnell, 2020.

This is a work of fiction. Similarities to real people, places, or events are entirely coincidental.

OFFICE OF SCIENTIFIC OPERATIONS - RELEASE #1

First edition. March 28, 2020.

ISBN: 979-8230207368

Written by K McConnell.

1

The two men, bundled in their winter gear, stood next to the communication building. Behind them, with a radio strapped to his back, stood a third individual manning the portable radio. They watched and waited. They were observing "Operation Experiment", a test explosion of a hydrogen bomb in the Arctic region of Baffin Island.

"By the way," said Professor Tom Nesbitt, a physicist from the Atomic Energy Commission, "where are the OSO guys?"

Colonel John Evans, military liaison, waved a mitten covered hand towards a truck twenty yards away. "They're in one of the trucks."

Nesbitt nodded. He didn't really see a reason for the OSO to be present for this. It was an important operation, but not typically the type of thing the OSO was involved in. He didn't, though, object to their being here. The OSO had proven itself in the past to be very important. There was no better example of that then the whole business with Dr. Zeitner and his army of prehistoric creatures back in the 30s.

In the truck sat Elliot Simms, District Chief Investigator for the OSO. He was of medium build, dark brown hair and a serious look to his features. Also in the truck was Robert "Robbie" Regan, District Investigator for the OSO. He was a little taller than Simms with sandy blonde hair and a brighter, cheery look to him.

Regan sighed. A stream of mist made a plume in front of his face in the cold air. "Why are we here again?" He asked.

Simms pulled the left side of his hood back so he could see Regan. "Because Marcus told us to." Simms said. Marcus Edmonds was the Director of the OSO.

"That's an order, not a reason." Regan replied.

"Well, the OSO is always interested any time atomic energy is used for something. You know, ever since—-" Simms was cut off.

"I know. Ever since the infamous Dr. Z." Regan waved a hand. They slid their goggles on.

The countdown to the bomb blast reached zero and a massive flash of light bathed the whole area. There was a tremendous roar, even at this distance, followed by several other rumblings.

Simms and Regan pulled their goggles off in time to notice Evans and Nesbitt hurry back into the communication building. Simms and Regan exchanged a look and shrugged. They climbed out of the truck and headed back into the communication building.

Inside Simms made his way to the coffee machine in an endeavor to warm up. A minute later Regan joined him. Simms glanced across the room where Colonel Evans, Nesbitt and the other physicist from the Atomic Energy Commission, Dr. Ritchie, were talking.

"Hey," Regan said as walked up to Simms, "the radar guys say they saw something right after the blast."

"Saw what?" Simms asked over the rim of his cup.

Regan shrugged. "They don't know. Something big, but no idea what it was. Then it was gone."

"Probably nothing. Maybe just debris." Simms said.

Regan nodded. "That's what they were thinking too."

Nesbitt strolled over to where Simms and Regan stood. "Ah, that coffee looks good."

Simms stepped aside so Nesbitt could get his own cup. "Anything to warm back up."

Nesbitt nodded. "Oh, we are planning to head out to the forward observation posts in about an hour."

"OK. Thanks." Simms replied. "Oh, Dr. Nesbitt, what post are we assigned to?"

Nesbitt flipped through a couple pages on his clipboard. "Uh, you two are at Post 13."

"Thanks." Simms said.

Turning back to them Nesbitt said, "Don't forget your Geiger counters. You'll need to keep an eye on the radiation levels."

Simms nodded. "Right."

Regan turned towards a soldier behind him. "Sergeant Loomis."

"Yes sir?" Loomis looked up from a pile of papers he was sifting through.

"Has transport been arranged for us?" Regan asked.

"Yes sir. It's all set." Loomis replied.

Regan nodded a thanks.

It took about 40 minutes of negotiating their way around crevasses and large jumbles of ice before the tracked vehicle carrying Simms and Regan drew near Post 13.

"This is about as close as I can get." The driver called over his shoulder to Simms and Regan.

"OK, we'll walk the rest of the way." Simms replied. They climbed over the side and out of the vehicle.

"Walk? More like crawl." Regan said staring at the piles of broken ice chunks, some larger than cars, blocking their path ahead.

Simms patted Regan on the shoulder and they headed off through the ice. After the first line of rubble blocking their path the ice smoothed out a little and they made better progress. Regan walked a little ahead of Simms who followed in the same footsteps until suddenly Regan wasn't there. One moment he was and then, gone.

It took Simms only a moment to realize that Regan had dropped into a crevasse. Hidden by snow they were easy to stumble into. Simms quickly dropped down on to his stomach and crawled up the edge of the crevasse which was visible now that Regan revealed it—-albeit, the hard way.

At the edge Simms was relieved to discover that a quick thinking Regan had buried his ice ax into the top lip of the crevasse as he slid into it. Hanging by one hand holding the ice ax Regan looked up at Simms.

"Sorry, Boss."

Simms planted his own ice ax several feet back form the edge and, gripping his own ax in one hand, reached down with his other hand and pulled Regan back up over the edge.

"I thought you were watching for those." Simms said waving a hand towards the crevasse as the both sat on the edge.

"I thought so too. Guess I better try a little harder." Regan replied as they stood up and, leaping carefully over the crevasse, continued their trek.

"I would like to be making better time than this." Simms said. "They were talking about a blizzard possibly heading our way."

"I think it's just over this next pressure ridge." Regan pointed on ahead.

They cleared the pressure ridge and spotted the flag marking the location of the post.

"Wait." Simms said.

Regan stopped and turned around to see Simms checking the Geiger counter.

"We're OK. Go ahead." Simms waved Regan on.

They reached Post 13. Simms opened the door of the instrument box and pulled out the circular paper disk that recorded data readings by etching them into the paper.

"Got it." Simms said. There was a sharp sound from somewhere, but the wind had picked up and was swirling around them.

"Did you hear that?" Regan asked.

Simms nodded. "I did, but with all this wind I can't tell where it came from."

They stood for a minute listening. They didn't hear anything.

"We better head back." Simms said.

They had only traveled a short distance more when they felt the ground shaking. They slid to their knees and waited for it to pass.

"What was that?" Regan asked.

Simms shook his head. "Don't know."

"This ground is slippery enough without it jumping around." Regan said.

"Agreed." Simms replied.

They stood up and after a few more steps heard what sounded like a gun shot. They exchanged a look and pushed on. Again, they only made a little progress before another more intense shaking of the ground knocked them down. Glancing back and to their right the two men saw a pressure ridge a short distance from them shift and break apart. It threw snow into the air that the wind spun around. It was like a fog. In the fog, though, something large and dark moved. It moved in a serpentine fashion. Like a snake or lizard, but a hundred times larger.

The wind picked up and the dark shape disappeared into the swirling snow. Both men looked at one another.

"Did you see...something?" Regan asked.

"I'm...not sure. Maybe." Simms said.

"Should we go investigate?" Regan asked.

Simms hesitated. "No. That direction heads out towards the open ocean. If we weren't careful we could end up dropping into the sea. If that happened...well..."

"Yeah. I get it." Regan answered.

Simms waved a hand. "Let's get moving."

A short time later they reached the tracked vehicle.

"Glad you guys are back. Something's happened." The driver told them.

"What happened?" Simms asked.

"Not sure." The driver replied. "A lot of chatter going on over the radio. Can't make it out."

The storm made the trip back to the base camp much longer. Once they were back and were headed towards the Communications building Simms stopped Regan.

"Don't say anything about what we saw out there." Simms said.

Regan looked puzzled. "Why? I mean, we did see something, didn't we?"

"Did we?" Simms asked. "For now, I want to keep that to ourselves. Understood?"

Regan shrugged. "OK. I guess."

They continued on into the building. There seemed to be people hustling all about. Regan flagged down Sergeant Loomis.

"What's going on?" Regan asked.

"It's doctors Nesbitt and Ritchie. Some kind of avalanche. Dr. Nesbitt is injured and they can't find Dr. Ritchie." Loomis answered.

"Can't find him?" Simms asked.

"Yes sir. Don't know where he is. Could be lost in the storm. They're sending guys out right now to search for him." Loomis said.

"How is Dr. Nesbitt?" Simms asked.

Loomis shrugged. "Not sure. It's weird, though."

"What's weird?" Regan prompted.

"Dr. Nesbitt. When he was brought in. He was mumbling something about a monster." Loomis gave a half shrug and was off.

Simms and Regan looked at one another. A monster?

2

After a brief phone call back to headquarters in DC it was decided that Simms and Regan would stay at the Baffin Island facility and do a little more investigating into what happened. Simms had described their encounter with something they couldn't really define to Edmonds. Marcus thought about it and agreed they should keep that to themselves for now. He also suggested that they talk to Colonel Evans about not mentioning what Nesbitt had said. The OSO did not want anyone thinking this was related in some way to events more than 20 years ago.

It took two full days for the blizzard to pass. To their credit the soldiers under Colonel Evans command struggled through the wild winds and blinding snow to search for Dr. Ritchie, but to no avail. No sign of him was ever found.

During the down time waiting for the storm to pass Simms and Regan spent their time interviewing anyone that had been out on the ice that day. They were trying to determine if anyone had seen something odd. They were careful not to suggest to anyone that something strange had taken place. In addition, they tried to dampen any rumors floating around that anything out of the ordinary happened.

"Colonel Evans." Simms pulled Evans aside at one of the brief moments he wasn't out on the ice himself or running around organizing search parties.

"Ah, Simms. Is it Mr. Simms? Do you guys have a rank? I never know with you government guys." Evans said with a smile.

"I'm referred to as District Chief Investigator—-DCI Simms." Simms answered.

"DCI Simms. OK. That works. What can I do for you?" Evans asked.

Simms hesitated. "I...don't wish to interfere in...your business, but after discussing what Dr. Nesbitt was talking about...the monster thing, the OSO feels like it would be best to not mention that to anyone. At least, for now. It's just that we at the OSO are a little sensitive to saying anything about monsters. I don't know how familiar you are with the events back in the thirties."

Evans nodded a little. "I heard about that stuff. A little before my time, though."

"Mine too." Simms agreed.

Evans patted Simms on the shoulder. "Well, not to worry. I had no intention of asking for a Section 8 by telling them back in Washington about monsters running around up here." With that Evans was off.

The following day Simms and Regan ventured back out to Post 13. They spent a good part of the day climbing around the ice debris fields in the general vicinity trying to find anything that would give them a clue what they might have seen. By the time they had returned to the base they were almost convinced that they had shared a hallucination borne out of swirling snow and wind.

The next afternoon Simms and Regan were catching a flight south on an Army transport, but weather conditions in Labrador, a stopover on the trip back, were bad and forced them to wait another 24 hours.

Landing in Labrador the two OSO agents checked into a hotel. They were scheduled for a flight to New York the following morning.

"Finally, real food." Regan said with a smile when their food arrived as they sat in the hotel restaurant.

Simms nodded. "Agreed."

They dug into their food and voices from two tables away could be heard rising slightly.

"I tell ya," One voice said, "it was like the whole ocean was comin' alive."

"I know, I know, I seen it too." A second voice confirmed.

Simms and Regan looked up from their meals at each other and then at the neighboring table.

"Somethin' big was goin' on out there." The first voice said.

"Like one of them maelstroms." The second voice added.

Reluctantly both Simms and Regan set their forks down, eased out of their chairs and walked over to the other table.

"Excuse me." Simms said politely. "It sounds like you have experienced something very unusual."

The two older men eyed Simms and Regan suspiciously.

"We're always looking for new and exciting stories for our magazine." Regan suggested.

The old men smiled slightly. "Well, we got a story for you then." One of them said.

"May we sit down?" Simms asked, already pulling out a chair.

"Sure enough." The second man said. "Are we gonna be famous?" He asked.

Regan shrugged. "You never know. So, what's your story."

"Well," The first man started, "we was out on a run."

"Along with the rest of them around here." The second man offered.

"Right." The first man continued, "Maybe twenty miles out, maybe more. We was out there fer a while when it started. You could see it further out. Waves."

"Well, it's an ocean." Regan remarked.

The first man shook his head. "this day the sea was gentle. Easy swells. And these waves...they were funny lookin'."

"Funny how?" Simms asked.

"They was just in one spot." The second man volunteered.

"Right." The first man agreed. "The waves weren't building. Like weather comin' in. No sir. This was just one spot out there where waves just rose up and not regular waves. They was moving in circles."

"And the splashing." The second man jumped in.

"Right." The first man nodded. "There was these giant geysers. Water just shootin' up into the air. Way up. Somethin' crazy was going on out there."

"And the boats." The second man offered.

"I was gettin' to that." The first man admonished the second. "A few of the others decided to go out and take a look. I think they was thinkin' maybe there was a big school out there. Not me. No sir. Never seen any schoolin' like that."

"Then they were gone." The second man couldn't hold back.

The first man frowned at the second. "Yep. We watched 'em go out and when they got close they just went under."

"Went under?" Regan asked.

Both old men nodded. "Gone." The first man said. "One minute they was there and then gone."

"Did you see what happened to them?" Simms tried to clarify what they were saying.

"No sir." The first man answered. "We saw...shapes."

"Shapes?" Regan prompted.

"Shapes. Big shapes. Dark shapes." The second man replied.

"What did the shapes look like? Could they have been just waves?" Simms asked.

The first man sighed and shook his head. "Mister, if those were waves, well, they ain't like any wave I ever seen in all my years of fishin'."

"Me either." The second man agreed.

There was a momentary pause.

"Were you able to save any of the men on those other boats?" Regan asked.

Both men slowly shook their heads.

"No sir." The first man said quietly. "Not single man returned."

With a solemn thank you Simms and Regan retreated back to their table. The next morning they caught their flight back to New York and from there on to DC.

3

"Are you Dr. Reynolds?" Simms asked the man.

The man, in his tweed jacket and tie, looked up from his desk. "Yes?"

Simms walked across the office with his hand extended. Regan followed him in.

"I am DCI Elliot Simms. From the OSO. We talked briefly on the phone."

"Oh, yes, of course." Professor Alton Reynolds, professor of Paleontology at the University which was conveniently located a short distance from the DC headquarters of the OSO, stood up and shook Simms' hand.

Simms turned. "This is DI Regan." Regan shook hands with Reynolds.

"Please sit. You had some question about prehistoric life I believe?" Reynolds said sitting back down.

Simms and Regan sat. "Yes," Simms replied, "we have a rather strange question for you."

Reynolds, a short slightly balding man in his early forties smiled at them. "Excellent. I love strange questions. They are the backbone of science, you know."

"Well, I think this is a doosy." Simms smiled briefly at Reynolds. "Is it at all possible for a creature to be frozen for a period of time and then...come back to life?"

Reynolds gave them an odd look. "Of course."

"Really?" Regan asked surprised. It wasn't the answer they were expecting.

"Certainly. It's been done before on several occasions." Reynolds said.

Simms was about to say something and then his thoughts changed direction. "Ah, I mean naturally. Not as the result of some...unauthorized scientific experiments."

Reynolds hesitated. "I'm not sure I understand exactly what you are referring to, but the answer is still yes."

Simms sat back. He glanced over at Regan. They had been prepared to be laughed out of the professor's office.

"So an animal can be frozen and then thousands or even millions of years later they thaw out and start roaming around again?" Simms asked.

Reynolds laughed a little. "Oh goodness no."

"But you just said..." Regan started.

Reynolds waved a hand. "No, no. Gentleman I was referring to frogs and fish and other such creatures. It has been proven that you can freeze these animals solid as a brick and slowly allow them to thaw back out and they will revive. But millions of years? No, I'm sorry gentlemen. That is not possible."

"Not even with the use of something like...atomic energy?" Simms asked the question carefully. It was not common knowledge about the diabolical work of Dr. Zeitner in the 30s and the crazy time that was.

It was known in the OSO because it ended up being their work that finally stopped Zeitner.

"Atomic energy?" Reynolds sat back in his chair. He thought for a moment. "Seems like I heard about some work done in that regard some time ago." He thought for a moment more and shook his head. "No. I...don't see how that would work. I am not an expert in atomic energy and I understand that they are discovering new and wonderful uses for it every day, but it seems unlikely it would work in this way."

Simms gave a short nod and stood up. He extended a hand out to Reynolds. "OK. Well, thank you Dr. Reynolds."

Reynolds stood up and shook Simms' hand. "Certainly. Any time." Reynolds watched them reach the door. "Oh, you know, you could talk to Dr. Neimens. In the Biology Department. I understand he has done some work in the use of radiation on living tissue. Perhaps he can shed more light on whatever it is you are trying to understand."

Simms nodded. "Thank you, Dr. Reynolds. We'll do that."

"You think it's worth our time talking to this Dr. Niemens?" Regan asked as they made their way down the hall of the University.

Simms shrugged. "Can't hurt. We're already here."

It took them a couple of wrong turns and a little help from students wandering the halls to find the office of Dr. Niemens. They walked in, explained to the secretary who they were and were ushered into Dr. Niemens' office.

"Dr. Niemens?" Simms asked as he and Regan entered.

"Yes?" The tall slender, dark haired man with a swarthy appearance responded.

Simms introduced the two of them, explained their question and Dr. Reynolds' recommendation to consult with him.

"Reanimate a deceased animal?" Niemens asked.

Simms nodded. "Yes. Is it possible?"

Niemens was quiet for a moment. He slid into a lab coat that had been hanging on a coat rack near his desk.

"Gentlemen, if you will come with me." Niemens said ushering them out the door of the office.

Simms and Regan followed Niemens down the hall, around a couple of corners and then through a door marked "No Admittance". Inside was a small laboratory. There was a variety of chemical equipment and instruments covering several tables. Niemens directed then to a particular table. A young lab assistant was making notes about something. The young man stepped back.

"Take a look at this." Niemens pointed towards a petri dish on the table.

Simms and Regan stepped up to the table. They leaned over and stared at a gooey blob inside the dish. They both looked over at Niemens.

"You are looking at living prehistoric flesh." Niemens said with a certain amount of undisguised pride.

"You mean like a dinosaur?" Regan asked.

Niemens shook his head. "That is not a dinosaur. It is a Woolly Rhinoceros. It was found by some Inuit people in Northern Canada frozen in the tundra."

"And you revived it?" Simms asked.

Niemens nodded. "With the help of a bit of radioactive material."

"So an atomic blast could revive a prehistoric creature? Like a dinosaur?" Simms asked.

Niemens looked skeptical. "I doubt it. This specimen is less than a million years old and it is just a chunk of flesh that is barely clinging to life. What you are talking about is something almost a hundred million years old and a complete animal. No, DCI Simms, I would find it difficult to believe an entire animal could be resurrected in such a fashion."

All three of them stared down at the petri dish.

"But not impossible?" Simms suggested.

Niemens gave an indulgent smile. "Well, maybe not impossible. Even so, such a creature could only survive for a short period of time. Eventually the radiation would consume the animal."

"Still," Regan said pointing at the dish, "that's amazing."

Niemens sighed. "Thank you. If only more of the scientific community felt as you do I could secure the funding such research deserves."

"I'm sorry Professor, we can't help you with that, but we do thank you for your time." Simms said.

Simms glanced at his watch as he and Regan made their way out of the building.

"We'll need a bit of luck in this evening traffic to make it back to headquarters in time for our meeting with the Director."

"Oh boy, can't wait. I'm sure the Director's going to have a field day with this tall tale." Regan said.

Simms shrugged. "Maybe. Maybe not. He's seen a few things in his time and he has a few tall tales of his own from when he was in the field."

4

The OSO offices in DC were clean and neat, but definitely not lavish. Practical would be the best term to describe them. There was a conference room, the Director's office, divided into the small reception area manned by the strawberry blonde and petite Jennifer and Marcus' actual office and the general office where the agents had their desks. One other room, perhaps the most important, completed the OSO offices. It was the communications room which was staffed 24 hours a day by three young officers on loan from the Army. The senior communications officer was Corporal Ridley.

Marcus Edmonds, Director of the OSO, was a man in his early fifties. He was stocky, well dressed with silver hair and a perpetual look of concern on his face.

Marcus stood at the head of the large oval table in front in the conference room. On the table in front of him was an array of papers. They were various reports he had been receiving from the military and his many contacts in the radio and newspaper industries.

Simms and Regan sat on one side of the table. Across from them sat DI Thomas Wayne and DI Jonathon Wyatt, the more junior pair of OSO agents.

"Well, gentlemen, do we or do we not have something going on?" Marcus waved at the papers in front of him. "The events of the past few weeks would certainly suggest there is something happening out there."

"But what?" Regan asked.

"Indeed." Marcus agreed.

"Professor Nesbitt believes that Project Experiment has unleashed some kind of prehistoric beast, but Dr. Reynolds, the paleontologist at the University, says it's not possible." Simms said.

"And Niemens, the biologist." Regan added.

"Right." Simms nodded.

Marcus was thoughtful. "Perhaps. Based on past events I would not entirely rule it out. Nonetheless, we cannot currently explain this." He waved at the papers on the table.

"And, well, we think we saw something." Regan said somewhat reluctantly.

"Yeah. What did you see?" Wyatt asked. He was a lean, brown haired guy in his late twenties.

"We're not sure." Simms answered for Regan.

"If you did see something," Wayne, a dark haired quiet, very deliberate young man, spoke, "then is it possible it could be the creature Dr. Nesbitt claims to have seen?"

"A good question." Marcus said.

Simms thought for a moment, then shook his head. "I doubt it. What we saw, if we actually saw it, moved quickly into the adjoining sea. It didn't seem to come from the direction of Posts 16, 17 or 18 which was the vicinity of Professors Ritchie and Nesbitt. I cannot say for certain, but I don't think this was their beast."

"You mean a second monster?" Wyatt asked.

Simms shrugged. "I don't know. I don't know that there were any monsters."

The agents were quiet for a moment and looked over at Marcus. He stood silently with his head bowed. He seemed to be weighing something.

"And what do we know about this 'maelstrom' that the fishermen from Labrador described?" Marcus asked.

Simms shook his head. "Nothing more than the Canadian Fisheries Department acknowledges the loss of several fishing vessels in what they refer to as an 'oceanic event'."

"Hmm, not very helpful, is it?" Marcus said.

"No. Not really." Simms agreed.

Ridley, the communications officer, appeared at the door. Marcus waved him in.

"Yes?" Marcus asked.

"Coast Guard Station 37, at Cape Cod, reports the remains of several whales have washed up on the shore." Ridley read from a slip of paper.

"OK. Thank you Corporal." Marcus looked around the table as Ridley retreated from the room.

"Well, yet another oddity." Marcus said. "Gentlemen, we have a few too many strange happenings for this to not warrant our full attention."

The agents nodded in agreement.

"Elliot, you and DI Regan take a look at Cape Cod. I want to know if this could be something natural or..." Marcus trailed off.

"A giant prehistoric predator?" Regan offered.

Marcus glanced at Regan. "Yes. Something along those lines."

"Yes sir." Simms said.

"DI Wayne and DI Wyatt, I understand that Professor Nesbitt has paid a visit to Dr. Elson in New York. He is the foremost paleontologist we have. If anyone might give us some further insight into what we are dealing with perhaps he could. I want you two to check in with him and see what the outcome of their meeting was."

"Yes sir." The two men agreed.

"Alright. Let's get on this. I am afraid things may start moving more rapidly." Marcus said and with that the meeting was adjourned.

As Marcus reached for the door knob of his office the phone on Jennifer's desk rang. Marcus hesitated.

"Office of the OSO." Jennifer said. It was a standard greeting, but anyone calling that number already knew who they were dialing. The phone number was not public and there weren't many people in the United States that had the number.

"Your name is Colonel Evans?" Jennifer confirmed as she looked over at Marcus. He thought for a moment and then stepped over to Jennifer's desk. He reached for the receiver.

"Yes sir. One moment please." Jennifer handed the phone to Marcus.

"This is Edmonds." Marcus said.

"Yes, Colonel, I know who you are."

Marcus laughed. "No sir. We don't keep tabs on everyone. I am familiar with your work on Project Experiment. How can I help you?"

"Uh, yes, I know about Dr. Nesbitt's claims concerning a prehistoric monster. I understand he has been talking to Dr. Elson, in New York."

"Does he now? That's...interesting. Dr. Nesbitt has convinced Dr. Elson that such a creature exists. And what are your thoughts on this prehistoric monster business?"

"Yes, it is a bit fantastic."

"Well, I agree it is wise to keep an open mind."

"Have we heard anything? Well we are somewhat concerned about some of the activities going on in the North Atlantic."

"I agree. Keeping an open line of communication is probably in the best interests of both of us."

"I will. I will keep you up to date on anything we discover."

"Very good. Thank you Colonel Evans." Marcus handed the receiver back to Jennifer and retired to his office.

5

Simms and Regan walked out along the beach. They could smell the stench of the carcasses long before they drew close to them. They stopped a short distance away. It was about as close as their stomachs would tolerate.

"Wow." Regan said holding a hand in front of his face.

Simms nodded. "Yeah."

They studied the whale remains for a few minutes.

"At first," Simms said, "I thought these just looked like they had been chewed on, but now..."

"More like they were just bitten in half." Regan added.

"Exactly." Simms said edging a little around part of the body.

"Can I help you?"

Simms and Regan turned around to see a Coast Guard officer had come behind them. Simms introduced them.

"Ah, yeah, they told me you guys would be showin' up." The officer said.

"How many whales do they believe are here?" Simms asked.

"The guys from Harvard tell me about 3 or 4. Kinda hard to tell since they are pretty butchered up." The officer answered.

"I see a lot of other stuff washed up here as well." Regan said pointing to debris scattered all along the shoreline.

The Coast Guard officer nodded. "Yeah. Looks like at least a couple of boats were wrecked out there too. We're going through it now to see if we can determine who they were. Also checking with the locals here to see who might be missing. We've got a ship out there searching for survivors right now."

Someone called to the Coast Guard officer and he wandered off.

"So, I guess the next question is: Is there anything in the ocean that can bite a whale in half?" Simms said returning his gaze to the mutilated whale.

"You mean besides a huge prehistoric creature brought back to life by an atomic blast?" Regan asked.

"Yes." Simms looked at Regan with a sideways glance. "Besides that."

Regan shook his head. "I'm no zoologist, but I'm guessing there isn't anything even close to big enough to do that." He pointed at a carcass where everything past the blow hole of the whale was gone.

Simms nodded. "I'm afraid I'd have to agree with you. And what that suggests is frightening."

They started walking back up the beach. An old man further along waved them over.

"Can we help you?" Simms asked.

"You G-Men?" The grizzled old guy asked.

Simms and Regan exchanged glances.

"We work for the government." Simms replied.

"Thought so. You look like 'em." The old man said nodding slightly. "You mind tellin' me what the government's plannin' to do about them things?"

"What things?" Regan asked.

The old man waved out towards the ocean. "Them things out there."

Simms eyes narrowed. "Did you see something out there?"

The old man shrugged. "Not sure I seen 'em, but I sure heard 'em. Made a hell of ruckus."

"What did you hear?" Regan asked.

"Two days ago. I was out here. Maybe early evenin'. It was just gettin' dim out. Heard water crashing about. Big water. Like a wave hittin' the shore. Only it was out there a good ways. Water was shootin' into the air and that sqawlin'..." The old man shook his head.

"Sqawling?" Simms asked.

"Yeah sir. Like nothin' I ever heard before. Sounded like a giant cat fight. Never heard nothin' make them kinda sounds before. Right out there." The old man pointed off to sea.

"But you didn't see anything?" Simms asked.

The old man shook his head. "Too far out. Lightin' was too dim. Saw somethin'. Shapes. Big shapes, but couldn't tell what they was."

"More than one shape?" Regan asked.

The old man hesitated. "I reckon there was. Can't say for sure, but I'm thinkin' more than one."

Regan and Simms looked at one another.

"Got them guys too." The old man said sadly.

"What guys?" Simms asked.

"Harley Madison and his helper Jimmie." The old man waved at some pieces of debris on the shore. "I recognize the markings. That's their boat. They go out night fishin' off here."

"Well, please let the Coast Guard officer up the beach know about the boat." Simms said.

The old man nodded still staring at the assorted junk rolling slightly in the surf.

"Gotta do somethin' about them things." The old man said as Simms and Regan turned and walked away.

6

"He's right in here." Lee Hunter, Dr. Elson's former student and current assistant, said as she ushered DI Wayne and DI Wyatt into Dr. Elson's spacious office. "He's very busy right now preparing for his dive."

"Dive?" Wayne asked.

"Yes, my dear boy. A dive!" Dr. Elson, a short round white haired and cheery looking man had suddenly materialized behind the two OSO agents.

Wayne and Wyatt turned around and shook hands with Elson.

"Yes, a dive. Why, I haven't been on one in years." Elson seemed quite delighted.

"What are you going diving for?" Wyatt asked.

"Why a Rhedosaurus. Can you believe it?" Elson scooted over to his book shelf. "Now where is it?"

"What are you looking for?" Lee came up beside Elson.

"Oh, Binghamton's volume of crest structures in Jurassic saurians." Elson said, randomly pulling out books from the shelf, examining them and piling them onto an adjacent table.

"It's right here." Lee reached past him and pulled it down.

"A Rhedosuarus?" Wayne asked.

"Huh," Elson looked over at Wayne. "Oh, yes. A Rhedosaurus. The lovely beastie that Dr. Nesbitt was so kind to find for us."

"Ah, so you know what the creature is, then?" Wyatt asked, he was excited at having come up with an important piece of information to take back to headquarters.

"Yes, yes, a Rhedosaurus, for sure, my boy. Well, we have to confirm it of course. That's what the dive is all about." Elson said as he started rifling through his desk drawers.

"Now what is it?" Lee asked Elson.

"I shall need a notebook. Something not too big of course, there won't be that much room in the bell, but with enough pages in it. I expect to be taking a great many notes." Elson, not finding the notebook he was looking for in the desk began glancing around the office.

"I will go find you something." Lee said, patting Elson on the arm.

"Ah, very good. Thank you my dear." Elson said with a smile.

"So, how do you know where to look for this creature?" Wayne asked.

"Well, if this the Rhedosaurus then it is presumably heading down to it's ancestral home, the Hudson Submarine Canyons." Elson answered.

"Uh, where...are these Hudson Canyons?" Wayne started.

"Oh, they are right here. Just off the coast from New York." Elson answered.

Wyatt looked over at Wayne. "Well, Thomas, I guess this confirms it then. There is some kind of prehistoric creature on the loose. And, Simms and Regan did see something come out of the Arctic ice."

Elson perked up. "Oh, someone else saw it besides Dr. Nesbitt?"

"Yes, Professor." Wayne replied. "Two of our other agents were with Dr. Nesbitt at Project Experiment. They also saw some kind of beast slither it's way along the ice and into the ocean."

Elson had been staring at a topographical map of the sea floor. He stopped and turned towards Wayne.

"Did you say 'slithered'?" Elson asked, perplexed.

Wayne nodded. "That's how they described it."

Elson stood thinking for a moment. "That seems odd."

"What does?" Wyatt asked.

"Well, the Rhedosaurus' hip structured would be raised and spread, perhaps even cantilevered. Its general locomotion should be something more like a waddling lizard. I don't think it would be capable of anything like a slithering motion. Very odd." Elson said, his face puzzled.

Wayne and Wyatt exchanged looks.

"Do you think it's possible that two creatures were thawed out by the atomic blast?" Wayne asked.

Elson smiled. "That would be wonderful, would it not, but I'm afraid the odds of such an occurrence would be remote at best. Well, unless, of course, the creatures were engaged with one another for some reason at the time of their sudden freezing."

"Engaged? Like in what?" Wyatt asked.

Elson shrugged. "Oh, I have no idea, my dear boy." Elson leaned back over the maps on the table.

Wayne and Wyatt thanked Elson and bid him farewell. Elson mumbled a farewell and it was obvious he was lost in the planning of his dive.

7

Once again the OSO agents and Marcus gathered in the conference room at OSO headquarters. Marcus waved a hand at DI Wayne.

"Well, sir, Dr. Elson is planning a dive."

"A dive?" Marcus asked.

"A dive?" Simms repeated.

"Yes sir." Wayne continued. "He is going down in..." Wayne glanced at Wyatt who leaned over showing him some notes from a notebook. "...the Hudson Submarine Canyons."

"Where is that?" Marcus asked.

"Uh, I believe he said it was just off the coast from New York."

"Like New York city?" Simms asked.

Wayne nodded.

"And that's where Dr. Elson thinks the beast is heading to?" Simms continued.

Wayne nodded again. "Yeah. That's what he seemed to indicate."

Simms glanced over at Marcus. "That sounds pretty damn close to a large populated area."

Marcus nodded. "Pretty close."

"Oh and the slithering." Wyatt volunteered looking at Wayne.

"Ah, yeah." Wayne acknowledged.

"Slithering?" Regan asked.

"Yeah." Wayne said. "We told Dr. Elson about what you two saw after Project Experiment. About the dark shape that seemed to slither into the ocean. He said that the creature that Dr. Nesbitt saw, the...what was it?" Wayne looked over at Wyatt.

Wyatt glanced down at his notes. "A Rhedosaurus."

"Ah, yeah, this Rhedosaurus that Dr. Nesbitt saw wouldn't slither. He said something about its hips that it might waddle a little, but not slither." Wayne went on.

"So, do you two still think what you saw slithered?" Marcus asked.

Simms and Regan looked at one another. They both nodded slightly.

"Yeah. I kind of think 'slither' is the right word." Simms said.

Marcus sighed. "So, are we back to thinking there may be two creatures and not just one?"

"We asked Dr. Elson about that?" Wyatt chimed in.

Everyone sat quiet for a moment.

"And?" Marcus prompted.

"Oh, yeah, he seemed to think the odds of that happening were remote." Wyatt answered.

"Unless," Wayne added, "they were engaged in something at the time they were frozen. That was what Dr. Elson suggested."

"Like what?" Regan asked.

"Fighting?" Simms suggested.

Marcus shrugged. "Maybe."

"Wait." Regan slapped his hand down on the table. "The maelstrom. Off the coast of Labrador."

"And whatever that old guy on the beach witnessed." Simms added.

"What old guy?" Wyatt asked.

Simms told them about their encounter with the old man on the shore and what he heard and kind of saw.

"Whoa." Wyatt said. "So these prehistoric monsters are in the middle of a fight millions of years ago, they get an instant freeze, then millions of years later they get thawed out by an atomic blast and just pick right up where they left off."

"Hmm," Marcus said, "an interesting theory." He stared down at the table.

It was Simms that noticed Ridley approaching the door. He stood up at opened the door and took the piece of paper from Ridley.

"Colonel Evans just called to let us know about Dr. Elson going down in the diving bell, which we already knew, and... he says that a lighthouse off the coast of Maine was completely destroyed." Simms looked up from the message.

"When was that?" Marcus asked.

Simms glanced down at the message. "It looks like before the incident off the coast of Massachusetts.

Marcus nodded slightly. "Well, that does confirm Dr. Elson's theory that whatever is happening, it certainly seems to be moving south. In the direction of New York."

"Sir?" Simms asked, looking at Marcus.

"Yes?"

"Should we let Colonel Evans know about the possibility of a second creature?" Simms asked.

Marcus hesitated. "Not yet. We are not 100% certain of that and I believe Colonel Evans has enough to deal with in tracking the first beast."

The room was quiet for a moment.

"Elliot, I want you and DI Regan to do some reconnaissance work. I want the two of you to fly along the coast in the area of New York city. If we're lucky, given the amount of activity around the port of New York you may get a first hand look at this creature."

"That seems like a long shot." Regan said.

Marcus shook his head slightly. "I don't think so. If that thing is moving towards New York there are an awful lot of things it is bound to encounter. It will get harder and harder for it remain hidden for very long. Besides, if you do get lucky and spot it, I have an idea."

"Oh?" Simms prompted.

"Back during the latter stages of the war the OSO and the Coast Guard worked on a project together. It was called Neptune."

"Oh, I heard about that." Wayne said. "That was some kind of electric weapon."

Marcus nodded. "Yes. It was designed as an anti-submarine weapon. Basically, once an enemy submarine was detected the Neptune device, when activated, would fire off a powerful electrical charge. The metal submarine would attract it. Like a bolt of lightning. Only under the sea. If it struck an enemy submarine it would have crippled it by overloading its entire electrical systems."

"You're gonna try to shoot one of these creatures with that?" Wyatt asked.

"Wait." Regan chimed in. "These creatures aren't made of metal. What would attract the electrical bolt to them?"

"Well," Marcus said, "I am thinking we won't need to actually hit the creature to cause enough discomfort to the beast to drive it away. We might be able to keep it away from any populated areas."

"Ah, that makes sense." Wyatt said.

"I will put in a call to our main contact in the Coast Guard, Captain Jackson, and see if we can't arrange to get Neptune to New York. In the meantime," Marcus pointed at Wayne and Wyatt, "I want you two onboard that ship when Dr. Elson goes down in that diving bell. I want to know the moment he finds something—if he finds something."

"Yes sir." Wayne and Wyatt agreed.

8

DI Wayne and DI Wyatt tried hard to stay out of the way on board the ship. On deck in the rear of the vessel the men were busy preparing the diving bell. There were plenty of people to see Dr. Elson off on his dive. Captain Jackson of the Coast Guard, Colonel Evans, Dr. Nesbitt and, of course, Dr. Elson's assistant Lee.

The two OSO agents felt it was best to keep a low profile. They were merely observers. Wyatt stared off towards the distant horizon further out to sea while Wayne was watching as best he could the launch preparations.

The diving bell lifted off the deck and was eased out over the water. Slowly the cable lowered the bell into the water.

"Wait. What the hell is...?" Wyatt stood up on his tip toes as he studied the ocean.

"What?" Wayne said turning around to look at Wyatt.

"There's something out there." Wyatt pointed into the distance.

Wayne stared out to sea and then moved closer to Wyatt. "What are you talking about? Where?"

"It's...it's gone now." Wyatt said, his eyes still sweeping along the lightly rolling waves.

"What is gone?" Wayne asked.

"I saw something. I'm pretty sure anyway." Wyatt said looking over at Wayne.

"What did you see?" Wayne asked, growing slightly impatient.

Wyatt shook his head slightly. "I'm not sure, but it looked long and dark. Like it was moving through the water."

Wayne stared out at the ocean, but saw nothing.

"You think we should, I don't know, let somebody know?" Wyatt asked.

Wayne looked at Wyatt and shook his head. "No, I don't. What would we tell them? That maybe you saw something. And maybe you didn't. I think all this talk about prehistoric monsters has you seeing them everywhere."

"Maybe." Wyatt didn't sound convinced.

Time passed. Since they were not connected into the communication system with the diving bell they did not know how the search was going. Suddenly there was a lot of raised voices and people scrambling around.

Wayne and Wyatt worked their way towards the back. After getting as close as they could without getting in anyone's way they called out to Colonel Evans to find out what was happening. He informed them of the loss of the diving bell and that the ship was heading back to port as fast as possible. There was nothing they could do about Dr. Elson, but the entire ship was now in grave danger.

On the hasty trip back to port Wayne and Wyatt were told about Dr. Elson's confirmation of the Rhedosaurus and that they were all but certain it was the Rhedosaurus that destroyed the diving bell.

Upon reaching port Wayne and Wyatt put in a call to Marcus at OSO headquarters to let him know what had happened to Dr. Elson. In addition, at Wyatt's insistence, Wayne related Wyatt's possible sighting of something further out to sea.

Wayne hung the phone up. "He wants us to stay here. He's concerned that New York may be at the center of this. Also, we are to report to Simms and Regan about what you may have seen."

Wyatt smiled. "Ah, finally, someone believes me."

"Maybe." That was as much as Wayne would concede for the moment.

Marcus hung up the phone. He stared down at the telephone for a moment more before slowly walking out of his office.

Jennifer, watching Marcus walk past, started to say something, but changed her mind seeing him in deep thought.

Marcus walked into the conference room and studied a map of the Eastern Seaboard. Reluctantly he was coming to the conclusion that there were indeed two creatures roaming about. Even without definitive proof it was becoming undeniable. Assuming DI Wyatt did see something moving along the surface it obviously could not have been the same creature that was attacking the diving bell at nearly the same time.

For a moment Marcus was trapped in a flashback to events almost 20 years earlier, but he felt certain that this was not a repeat of that horror. He sighed and tapped on the map where the Hudson Submarine Canyons were. If the first creature, this Rhedosaurus, was headed into those canyons, where was the second creature going? He could only hope that DCI Simms and DI Regan's reconnaissance flight would provide some clue.

9

After takeoff the plane banked slowly to the south. The original flight plan had called for Simms and Regan to fly North and East along the Long Island shoreline, but the call from DI Wayne changed that. With confirmation of one of the creatures in the deep waters off New York City and Wyatt's possible sighting of something in the same vicinity heading south, it made little sense to look for anything to the north.

The plane was small. Simms sat on the left side peering out a window. Regan was on the right side. They were high enough to take in a large swath of ocean, but low enough to, hopefully, spot something out of the ordinary.

Just south of New York ship traffic was fairly heavy. There seemed to be no visible issues between the numerous ships and smaller boats here and any giant prehistoric beasts. They flew further south keeping the Jersey coast clearly in sight on their right.

"There! What's that?" Regan said pointing at something below.

Simms moved to a seat behind Regan and stared down at the sea below.

"I don't see anything." Simms said.

"There. It's back again. Just back there." Regan pointed a little behind them.

Simms twisted in his seat. "Yeah. Looks like something. Not sure what, but definitely something long and dark. It's gone now."

They called up to the pilot and had him circle back around. They combed the area, going over it several times, but didn't get even a glimpse of the dark shape again.

"What do you think?" Regan asked looking back over his shoulder at Simms.

Simms shrugged. "Don't know. But I saw something. Something big."

Regan nodded. "Yeah."

"Not sure if it was the same thing we saw up at Baffin, but it could be." Simms said.

"I agree." Regan said.

The copilot leaned back, yelled something and waved at Simms. The plane started banking around and Simms stumbled a little trying to make his way forward.

"What is it?" Simms yelled over the noise of the plane to the copilot.

The copilot handed his headset over to Simms.

Regan leaned left a little to watch Simms talking to someone over the radio.

"What's up?" Regan asked as Simms returned to his seat.

"We've been ordered back to New York. That Rhedosaurus just came ashore. Right in the city."

"Holy crap." Regan said.

By the time they landed back in New York they could tell the southern end of Manhattan was devolving into chaos. They managed to convince a taxi driver to get them close to the Wall Street area before the streets became impossible to navigate with a vehicle. Getting out Simms and Regan worked their way to the backside of the Federal Building. At this point the screams of people was frightening. On a more subtle level there was a soft rumbling coming through the pavement at their feet that was equally unnerving because they had a feeling of what was making it.

They reached the front corner of the Federal Building after dodging panic stricken people fleeing Wall Street. They looked out past the building and stood motionless, stunned. It was easily four stories tall. Skin like armor plating, it moved in a waddling walk indiscriminately snatching people and cars up in a massive mouth filled with large sharp teeth.

"My God!" Regan gasped out. He pulled out his revolver.

Simms reached out and put a hand over Regan's gun. He shook his head at Regan's questioning glance.

"That won't do any good." Simms said over the roar of screams, sirens and destruction.

Regan glanced down at his gun and then back at the beast. He slipped the gun back under his coat.

"What do we do?" Regan asked.

Simms shook his head. "Nothing we can do. So we get the hell out of here."

They worked their way back several blocks. Spotting a small grocery store they ducked in and, showing badges, ousted a newspaper reporter from the pay phone. Miraculously they got through to Marcus at OSO headquarters. Simms described the scene in New York and what they saw in the plane further south. Marcus ordered them to find Colonel Evans who has been placed in charge of stopping the beast.

"So, how exactly do we find Colonel Evans in this mess?" Regan asked as they stepped back out on to the street.

Simms stood looking around and then pointed down towards an intersection two blocks north.

"That's how." Simms said.

Regan turned to look and saw a jeep stopped in the middle of the intersection and several soldiers, one armed with a bazooka, take up a position.

"Ah, good plan." Regan agreed.

After a couple of minutes of explanations and showing their credentials the two OSO agents were directed to a building back in the direction of the Federal Building from which they had fled earlier. Upon reaching the building they were told that Colonel Evans was up on the roof.

Simms and Regan walked out on to the roof. There were soldiers moving all around piling up sandbags, stringing wire and wrestling with small caliber artillery piece. The sun was just setting.

"Gentlemen. Nice of you to join our little party." Colonel Evans said greeting them.

"Quite a little set up you have going here." Regan said looking around.

"What made you decide on this location?" Simms asked.

"Well, we know the beast is somewhere around in this vicinity. We have good sights down several streets from here. With luck we'll get a shot at him." Evans replied.

Simms and Regan nodded.

Darkness fell and the soldiers, the ones on the roof and those behind barricades on the street below, waited and watched for the creature. At the sound of rumbling from one of the side streets that ended at the base of the building spotlights swung around and found the creature tentatively approaching.

Dr. Nesbitt and Lee Hunter joined them on the roof of the building and watched as Colonel Evans ordered the artillery to fire at the creature, but the shell only bounced off the thick skull of the beast. The soldiers in the street were able to injure the creature with a bazooka at close range as the monster attempted to breach some electrified wires spread out in front of the soldiers.

As quickly as the creature appeared it disappeared. One moment it was lighting up the dark street with electric shocks from the wires and then it was gone. Colonel Evans ordered the soldiers at street level to recon in an attempt to find where the beast went.

"What's going on?" Simms asked Evans as he walked past them.

"I'm heading back to the command center." Evans replied.

"I mean with the men. I overheard some of the soldiers saying something was making them sick." Simms said.

"Oh, that. Not sure. Something is affecting them. I've ordered the medics to check them out." Evans explained.

"Do you think the creature was seriously wounded?" Regan asked.

Evans shrugged. "Don't know. It was definitely bleeding though and that's a good sign. My guess is it's heading back towards the waterfront." With that Evans disappeared through the door to the steps.

Simms and Regan made their way back down to the street level of the building. Finding a pay phone Simms called Marcus and related the encounter with the creature and about the sickness that seemed to be affecting the soldiers.

"I don't like the sound of that." Marcus said.

"Maybe it is some kind of defense the creature uses when attacked." Simms suggested.

"Maybe." Marcus replied. "Or maybe the beast was not the only thing that was awakened when it was thawed out."

"What do you mean?" Simms asked.

"Well, there was presumably a very different ecosystem in place when this creature was frozen on that ice. It's possible that some kind of bacteria or virus that was living on or in that thing and it's now being spread around by the creature. Something we have never encountered before."

"Now I don't like the sound of it either." Simms said.

"Right. As it turns out I had already sent DI Wayne and DI Wyatt over to the hospital to talk to some of the people that witnessed the creature up close. I will have them inquire with the doctors there if they are seeing anything similar." Marcus said.

"OK, what should we do?" Simms asked.

"Find Captain Jackson. Have him prepare the Neptune and be ready to launch with him as soon as possible. If Colonel Evans is right we need to catch this creature and kill it before it escapes out to sea again." Marcus replied.

"OK. We're on it." Simms hung up.

"Well?" Regan asked.

Simms looked at him. "Our turn to go sailing."

10

"Sorry, no one comes in." The soldier said. He held a rifle and blocked their path into the hospital.

"What's going on?" DI Wyatt asked.

"Doctor Leeds has ordered that the hospital go into quarantine." The soldier explained.

"Now, move it along." A second solider said stepping up next to the first.

DI Wayne pulled out his credentials and handed them to the first soldier. That soldier glanced at them and then handed them to the second soldier with a puzzled look. He understood what he was reading, but was clearly unsure whose authority outranked the other.

"What's an OSO?" The first soldier asked the second one.

"I don't know. I'll check inside." The second soldier said and disappeared back through the main door of the hospital. A couple of minutes later he reappeared.

"They said OK, but you gotta wear masks." The second soldier handed Wayne and Wyatt surgical masks.

Wayne and Wyatt looked at each other.

"So is it safe with just these on?" Wyatt asked the soldier.

The soldier shrugged. "Don't know, but if want to go in you gotta wear 'em."

The two agents donned the masks.

"Good luck." Said one of the soldiers as they walked through the hospital door.

"So, it's safe to say that whatever is making the soldier's sick is here too." Wyatt commented.

"Looks like it." Wayne replied.

"Is this a good idea? Being here now." Wyatt asked as they navigated the busy hall.

Wayne looked over at Wyatt. "Irrelevant. It's our job. We go where we have to. We go where others shouldn't. It's just the nature of the job."

"I guess, but putting on one of these masks makes me cringe every time I breathe." Wyatt said.

"It is a little creepy." Wayne replied.

They had to ask a couple of people and work their way up two floors before they finally found Dr. Stanley Leeds. Under the quarantine lock down, he was in charge.

They greeted Dr. Leeds and explained who they were.

"So is it possible to talk to some of the people that saw the creature up close?" Wayne asked.

Dr. Leeds shook his head. "I wouldn't recommend getting close to any of the patients that have the sickness. There are some whose injuries are not serious and do not show any signs of the sickness. You can talk to them if you want. The only problem is, we don't really know that they don't have the sickness and just aren't showing signs yet. No idea the incubation period of it. So, well, you can take your chances if you want, but if you do I will probably have to quarantine you as well."

Wayne and Wyatt looked at one another.

Wayne shook his head. "No, doctor. Being stuck here under quarantine is not an option for us. What can you tell us about the sickness?"

Dr. Leeds gave them a quick weary smile. "Honestly, gentlemen, I don't have time to get into that right now. Tell you what, I will have one of my assistants fill you in on what we know." He turned and called out. "Sam, can you come here."

"Yes, doctor?" Sam joined them.

"Fill these two gentlemen in on what we know about the sickness. Gentlemen, it was nice meeting you, but I need to get back to work."

"Sure, thank you doctor." Wayne returned.

It took about ten minutes for Sam to run through all that they had determined so far about the sickness. He apologized about not being able to answer all of their questions. They were a little shorthanded and their ability to thoroughly analyze the blood samples was limited here.

Wayne thanked him.

"So, what now?" Wyatt asked.

"We call it in." Wayne said and worked his way back to a nurse's station. He found a free phone and put the call through to OSO headquarters.

When Wayne hung up he turned to Wyatt. "He wants us to get one of the blood samples and get it to Washington right away."

"Why? I thought we were hunting prehistoric beasts?" Wyatt asked.

DI Wayne's face was serious. "The Director is concerned this new disease could turn into a pandemic."

"You mean like spread all around the world?" Wyatt's face held a trace of fear.

"Something like that." Wayne replied.

"And we gotta carry some of that stuff around with us?" Wyatt asked.

"Yup. So, you might want to watch your step." Wayne said.

"Thanks. Great advice."

11

At OSO headquartered Marcus had Jennifer work on tracking Colonel Evans down. It took her a little while, but eventually she found him at the facility designated as Area Command. She passed the phone over to Marcus.

"Colonel Evans?" Marcus asked.

"Yes, Director Edmonds." Evans replied.

"I appreciate you keeping my men appraised of the situation." Marcus said, always the diplomat.

"Well, we're all on the same team here. Speaking of which, it looks like we have some kind sickness going around up here and it seems to be coming from this creature." Evans said.

"I know about it. I have two of my agents at the hospital now. They are going to bring a blood sample here to Washington. We need to determine if this is going to be threat to the general population." Marcus said.

"Great. That's all I need is something else to worry about." Evans replied.

"I understand. All the more reason we need to determine the threat this new disease poses and, if need be, come up with some kind of vaccine against it." Marcus said.

"I agree." Evans said.

"Colonel, I have another idea that might help us." Marcus said.

"I'm all ears for anything that might help. What have you got?" Evans asked.

"Have you heard of the Neptune?" Marcus asked him.

"Neptune. Sounds familiar. Wait, isn't that the thing the Navy was working on to zap submarines?" Evans answered.

"Yes. We here at the OSO worked with the Coast Guard to build it. The original intent was to be able to neutralize enemy submarines during the war, but it was not completed in time to be used."

"OK." Evans' voice left a question hanging in the air.

"I think it might be useful to us now. If we could target the creature while it is still in the water we just might be able to kill it." Marcus explained.

Evans was quiet for a moment. "I'm not sure that's our best plan of action. I think the creature is seriously wounded. Hell he might even be dead now. But I want to be sure. I would prefer we kill him on shore so we can verify he's dead. If the Neptune can kill him—and we don't know that it will work—-he could end up dying somewhere down in those canyons offshore. We might never find his body and never know for sure if we got him. Despite the risk, I would rather he come ashore and give me another crack at him."

Marcus thought for a moment. "I see your point Colonel."

"I tell you what, though," Evans went on, "maybe the Neptune could drive the beast out of the sea and back up to us. And, once he does resurface, it could keep him from getting away again. We can keep him right up where we can pick him apart."

"Agreed. I have some men getting the Neptune ready now. I will have them take down into the lower bay and see if we can't drive your target back to you." Marcus said.

"Great. Have your men contact Area Command as soon as they are in position." Evans said.

"Very good." Marcus hung up and had Jennifer work on getting a call through to Captain Jackson. He hoped DCI Simms and DI Regan were close to having the Neptune ready.

12

Simms and Regan stood back and watched. They were impressed by the efficiency of the Coast Guard sailors as they secured the Neptune device at the stern of the small cruiser. It was essentially a thick inverted U shaped bracket with a winch at its base and metal arms that hung out over the back of the ship. A cable from the winch threaded up the bracket and out to the end of the metal arms. From there the cable went through a pulley and down to the device itself. The Neptune was a large silver ball with several large electrical cables coming out of the top of it. Inside the ball, sealed away, were capacitor plates and baffles that helped direct the massive electrical charge out through the bottom of the ball. The polarity of the Earth drew the charge downward and anything metallic along the way would further direct it. The primary knock against the Neptune was that it was not a weapon of precision. Like lightning, it tended to follow its own erratic path to its ultimate destination.

Once the Neptune had arrived at dockside it took just over an hour to get it in place and tested. The ship pulled out of port and, as it cleared the other boat traffic, hastily moved out into the lower bay, south of Manhattan.

Simms and Regan stood with Captain Jackson staring back at the Neptune as the ship approached the initial firing target. The deck felt oddly sloped down towards the Neptune.

"Have you ever seen this operating?" Jackson asked the two OSO agents.

They both shook their heads.

"Is there any risk to the people onboard?" Regan asked.

"Not unless you're wearing a suit of armor." Jackson replied with a smile. "Actually, this particular ship has a coating on the hull that gives it a neutral charge."

"That's comforting." Regan replied.

When the ship reached the coordinates for the initial firing. The Neptune was lowered into the water.

"How far down do you go with it?" Simms asked.

"Depends on how deep your target is estimated to be. In this case, we are assuming the beast is on the bottom. So, let's see, in these waters...maybe 100 feet." Jackson explained.

At the bow of the ship they heard the anchor chain clanging out.

"You're dropping the anchor?" Simms asked.

"Counter balance. This is a small vessel and the Neptune actually weighs quite a bit. Don't want it dragging us down." Jackson said.

"Yeah. Let's not do that." Regan agreed.

"Ready sir." One of the sailors called out.

"Fire when ready." Jackson answered.

A moment later there was powerful muffled buzzing sound. Water boiled up around the ship a little. The men onboard saw their hair raise up a slightly. The whole firing took no more than five seconds.

"Wow. I'm glad I'm not at the other end of that." Regan commented.

Jackson nodded.

The Neptune was pulled back up. The anchor was reeled in as well. The ship held its position for ten more minutes. They watched the sonar and the sea all around them for any sign that the Neptune had disturbed the beast.

"So...if we do, say, spook this monster out of its hiding place...what keeps this really pissed off creature from surfacing and coming after us?" Regan asked.

Jackson glanced at Regan. "Not a damn thing."

"I just love my job." Regan said shaking his head.

The ship moved further along the canyon and fired off the Neptune again. After waiting the appropriate amount of time or, as Regan put it, "Long enough to see if we get eaten", they moved again.

There was a deep shudder accompanied by the muffled buzzing and the weird tingling of static in the air signaled the third firing.

"I'm not sure you could ever get accustomed to that." Simms said quietly.

Jackson shook his head a little. "No, it doesn't seem like you do. It's too...strange."

The three of them stood waiting to see if the Neptune aroused anything. It was an odd waiting period. Just standing there to see if something monstrous rose up and potentially killed them.

Fast footsteps made all three men turn around. A sailor handed Captain Jackson a message. He read through it quickly and then called out an order to secure the Neptune and get the ship underway.

"What's going on?" Simms asked.

Jackson waved the piece of paper. "The creature just came ashore at Manhattan Beach. We are ordered to stand just offshore and make sure it doesn't try to get away again."

13

"Glad to have dropped that stuff off." Wyatt said as he and Wayne got out of the taxi that had just dropped them off at the University. "That was the longest trip back here to Washington I have ever taken."

"Well, that sample is the lab's problem now. We just need to talk to Professor Reynolds about this second creature." Wayne said as they entered the Science Building and made their way to the office of Dr. Reynolds.

Reynolds looked up from his desk as the two agents were escorted in by Reynolds' secretary.

"Gentlemen, please have a seat." Reynolds said pleasantly. He reached back and turned the volume of the radio down. He had been listening to news broadcasts from New York on the rampage of the beast.

"I spoke to your colleagues recently and, well, it seems they were right." Reynolds said.

"It does seem like we have a genuine problem on our hands. Are you aware that there are two creatures roaming about?" Wayne asked.

"Two?" Reynolds looked shocked. "Two of these prehistoric animals? Both awakened by an atomic blast?"

"So it seems." Wayne confirmed.

Reynolds shook his head. "The odds of such a thing is, well, incredible."

"Well, Dr. Elson believed that the beast in New York was returning to its natural habitat. The second creature, however, does not appear to be in the same area. It has continued, apparently, further south along the Atlantic coast. What we were hoping you could help us with was some idea on where this second creature was headed to." Wayne explained.

Reynolds was quiet for a moment with his head lowered slightly. "The loss of Dr. Elson is a great blow to all of us."

"Yes." Wayne agreed. He waited for Reynolds to continue.

Reynolds sighed. "Without knowing the species, well, it would be almost impossible to guess where this other animal is headed to."

"So, there's no way to know where to look for this creature?" Wyatt asked.

Reynolds didn't answer right away. "Did you say this second animal was moving along the coastline?"

Wayne nodded. "That appears to be the case."

"Not out to sea?" Reynolds asked.

Wayne shook his head. "We don't believe so. All sightings and encounters with the second beast have been almost within sight of the shoreline."

"Hmm, that's interesting. If it was just searching for food the deeper waters would make more sense for it. Or even the Grand Banks where it has already passed through. The fact that it is keeping closer to the shore suggests a different agenda." Reynolds said.

"Like it just wants to eat us?" Wyatt offered.

Reynolds laughed a little. "No, I hardly think we are of any interest to it. Remember we didn't even exist the last time this animal swam in these waters. No, it seems more likely it is seeking something."

"Like what?" Wayne asked.

"Well, we probably shouldn't over think this too much. If it's not food it's looking for then it is probably the other primary thing that drives animals. I think Dr. Elson's theory concerning the first of these animals holds true for the second as well." Reynolds said.

"You mean it's looking for a mate?" Wyatt asked.

"At least, its natural mating grounds." Reynolds replied.

"And where would that be?" Wayne asked.

Reynolds shrugged. "Who knows. But, I would think, the animal doesn't know either."

"Huh, it's been frozen for millions of years. It's probably long since forgotten the place." Wyatt said.

Reynolds shook his head. "Doubtful. This wouldn't be something it would have committed to memory. This is something that is instinctive. No, the problem for this animal is that the North American shoreline would have changed significantly since it last was here. I think it is just looking for something that looks similar to its original spawning grounds."

"That still doesn't really help us figure out where it's headed." Wayne said.

Reynolds nodded. "I would agree. I'm afraid we won't know its destination until the creature figures that out itself."

The two agents thanked Reynolds and headed back to OSO headquarters. They knew their news to the Director would not be well received.

14

Simms and Regan, after being shuttled to shore by Captain Jackson, were escorted through the throng of soldiers populating the grounds of Coney Island and to the front of the crowd where Colonel Evans and Lee Hunter stood watching the massive creature tear the roller coaster apart. They caught Evans' attention and he walked over to them and explained that Dr. Nesbitt thought the only way to be sure they killed the beast and not spread the sickness all over the place was to inject a radioactive isotope into it.

"So who's the lucky guy that's gotta walk up to that thing and poke it with a needle?" Regan asked.

Evans laughed a little. "That's not exactly our plan. We've got our best sharpshooter armed with a projectile on the end of a rifle."

"You think he can penetrate the hide of that thing?" Simms asked skeptically.

Evans shook his head. "Don't have to penetrate its armor. We nicked the thing with a bazooka at close range, remember. It's got a wound right here." Evans pointed to his collarbone.

"So he's got hit that one spot?" Simms asked.

Evans nodded. "Yeah. That's why we have are best marksman on it. Hell, if we could just hit the damned thing anywhere, I could've taken the shot. It's kinda hard to miss something that size."

"Can't argue with that." Regan said staring at the beast in the distance.

"I understand you got a close up view of the Navy's little toy." Evans said.

Simms nodded. "It's pretty impressive. I had read about its development, but hadn't ever seen it before."

"Well, it sounds like a hell of a thing. I'm sure it was responsible for pushing our friend here back up on to shore. I was sure it was going to hide in the depths until its wound healed. God knows when or where it would reappear. We don't have enough manpower to watch every inch of shoreline." Evans said.

Simms and Regan exchanged a look. They were instructed to inform Evans of the second beast.

"Yeah." Simms spoke slowly. "About watching the shoreline..."

"Hang on." Evans said, holding up his hand. "Looks like they are in position to take the shot. Excuse me." Evans walked forward out in front of the soldiers to where Lee Hunter stood. It had become obvious through this ordeal that Lee Hunter and Dr. Nesbitt had become involved. Now, with Dr. Nesbitt having volunteered to accompany the sharpshooter in moving up to take the shot, Lee was nervously watching.

Simms and Regan watched as Nesbitt and the sharpshooter rode a slow moving roller coaster car to the top of the roller coaster in order to get a shot at the creature, now not more than 200 feet away. The sharpshooter took his shot and hit directly into the wound. The beast thrashed about igniting a fire that began consuming the entire wooden roller coaster. Nesbitt and the sharpshooter were forced to climb down the roller coaster framework to escape the flames.

Lee Hunter embraced Nesbitt as he and the sharpshooter safely returned to the crowd of soldiers. In the distance the beast made several dying shrieks and finally slumped to the ground to the cheers of the gathered soldiers.

Simms slipped up next to Colonel Evans as he finished shaking Nesbitt's hand.

"Colonel." Simms said.

Evans turned to Simms with a smile. "Well, put that one down in the books. I am glad that's done."

"About that." Simms said. "We're not quite done."

"Huh?" Evans looked at Simms. "What do you mean?"

"Well, sir, we weren't sure until quite recently, but we are now certain there's a second creature." Simms said.

Evans stared at him for a moment. "What? A second one? What are you talking about? Where?"

Nesbitt stepped over to them. "Did I hear you say something about a second creature?"

Simms took a deep breath. "Yes sir. It seems this creature was not the only one that was awakened by the blast."

"Damn it. And you didn't think to mention this earlier?" Evans said, clearly pissed off.

"We weren't sure until very recently and, well, this creature was cornered here. We thought it would be best to focus on killing this one first. While we had the chance." Simms said.

Evans stood quietly fuming.

"He's right." Nesbitt chimed in. "You know he's right." Nesbitt spoke to Evans.

Evans nodded. "I know it, but I still should have been told immediately."

"Yes sir." Simms said quickly. "We wanted to be sure. We didn't want to confuse the situation if we weren't 100% certain."

"Fine." Evans said abruptly. "So where is this other creature?"

"Somewhere south. Along the Jersey shore. We've talked to Dr. Reynolds at the University in Washington, but we haven't been able to determine where it is headed." Simms answered.

It was agreed to get back to Area Command and put in a call to Edmonds at OSO headquarters. Edmonds brought Evans and Nesbitt up to speed on everything the OSO knew about the second creature. In addition, he let everyone know there was another ship reported lost along the Jersey coast.

As frustrating as this would be, it was decided that until the location of the creature could be determined the most they could do at the moment was begin to transfer their military men and equipment south in preparation for another confrontation.

15

"Wow, now that was somethin'." The guy said as the three of them emerged from one of the livelier jazz clubs in the late night hours of an Atlantic City night.

"They were layin' it down." The second guy said in agreement as the three of them began making their way north along the dimly lit street. Their steps were somewhat shaky, but the cool air of the night was helping a little towards sobering them up.

The three men stopped for a moment. From this spot they had a good view of the water as it flowed either in or out, depending on the tide, of the swampy salt marshes that lay between the mainland and Brigantine Island. Two of the men leaned with their backs against a railing while the third faced out towards the water.

"Whoa. What happened to the bridge?" The third man asked.

One of the other two waved a hand without turning around. "Oh, that bridge has been gone since a hurricane took it out years ago. You know that."

The third man, still facing the water, nodded. "Oh yeah. I remember now. Hey, was it the wind that took out that bridge or a wave."

"Hell, I don't know." One of the others replied.

"I thought maybe it was a wave, you know, like that one." The third man pointed out at the water.

The other two men turned around. Sure enough, they stared at a long rippling wave moving just now through the remaining pylons of the old bridge. They watched it not fully realizing that it was not a normal wave. Instead of being parallel to the shore it was perpendicular and clearly moving past the remnants of the bridge and into the salt marshes. Just before the wave moved out of their sight the three men watched something from the front of the wave lift up out of the water. They couldn't clearly make out what it was they were seeing, but they all agreed it was at least ten feet above the surface.

They looked at one another, hesitated and the backed slowly away from the railing. They moved further from the water and when they were a full block away a car turned the corner and slowly cruised in their direction. As the car drew closer they recognized it as a police car.

Without saying a word all three men began waving at the police to stop.

The policeman rolled his window down. "Is there a problem, gentlemen?"

The third man pointed back towards the water. "There's something out there."

"Out where?" The officer asked.

"The river. Something in the river." The second man answered.

"Something big." The first man offered.

The policeman sniffed the air. "Smells like you guys have been making a night of it, haven't ya?"

"There was something there." The third man insisted.

"It went into the marshes." The second man added.

"Past that old bridge." The first man tried to sound helpful.

The policeman smiled at them. "Tell you what, you guys go sleep it off and in the morning if you still see big things in the water we'll all go and have a look. OK?"

"But you gotta..." The second man started, but the officer waved his hand, rolled up his window and slowly drove away.

Later at the station the policeman stood at the front counter filling out a nightly report sheet.

"So McKinley, anything exciting tonight?" The Sergeant sitting behind the counter asked. In the background a radio was on.

"Nope. Just the usual. Drunks and bums." McKinley answered, not looking up from his report.

The music on the radio abruptly stopped and the stern voice of a man took over.

"This just in, the Coast Guard has issued an alert for the entire New Jersey coast. Be on the lookout for anything out of the ordinary. All citizens are asked to report any missing vessels, shoreline debris or large dark moving objects to the Coast Guard immediately. In addition, all citizens are urged to stay out of the ocean and away from the shore. There were no further details concerning this alert. Stay tuned to this station for more information as we receive it."

Officer McKinley's pencil stopped in midair over the sheet of paper. He glanced up at the Sergeant who was staring at the radio before turning to look back at McKinley.

"What do you make of that?" The Sergeant asked.

"I'm thinkin' maybe you should call the Coast Guard." McKinley said.

"Call the Coast Guard? Why?" The Sergeant stared at McKinley.

"Because I think some gentlemen I met earlier this evening may not have been as drunk as I thought."

16

"So what do you think?" Evans asked. The three of them stood looking out at the pylons of what was once the Brigantine Island bridge.

DCI Simms shook his head a little. "I honestly don't know, but Director Edmonds' hunches are often right so..."

Evans sighed. "I hope so because we are moving a lot of resources down here for nothing if it ends up being a wild goose chase."

Simms nodded without saying anything.

"That is one big swamp." Regan said. "Why would it want to go into that?"

"I don't know, but if it did we have an even bigger problem." Evans replied.

"What's that?" Simms asked.

Evans waved out towards the Absecon Swamp. "I studied the map last night. That place is big and I can't sail anything of any significant size in there."

"So you'll have to go in with small boats?" Regan asked, thinking of when they were in the lower bay firing off the Neptune and how small he felt on that boat.

Evans shook his head slowly staring out past the pylons of the old bridge. "I sure as hell wouldn't want to go hunting one of these beasts in a PT boat and I don't like the idea of having to ask for volunteers to go in there."

"Can't we just bring a battleship in to shell the swamp? We would either kill it or drive it back out into open water." Simms suggested.

Evans shook his head. "No. We don't know if this creature carries the same disease as the other one or not. If it does and we blow it to pieces, well, we don't want to do that. Besides that, one errant shell this close to Atlantic City might be just about as bad as that monster. It's just too populated around here."

"So what is the plan?" Regan asked.

Evans stared at the swamp in silence for a moment. "Surround it."

"Surround it?" Regan looked at Evans. "We don't know where it's at."

"Yeah we do." Evans pointed. "It's in there."

"You mean surround the whole swamp?" Regan asked staring out across the swamp.

Evans nodded. "Yup. All of it. The whole thing. I have enough men moving this way to cover the entire land side and the Coast Guard will blockade the routes leading back out to sea. Anywhere it tries go we'll be there."

"And then what?" Simms asked.

"Same thing we did with the first creature. We shoot it full of plutonium and kill it." Evans answered.

The three of them were silent.

"I think I should contact Professor Nesbitt and let him know we will need another plutonium shell." Simms said.

Evans gave a quick nod. "Ah, right, someone should speak to him. It will probably take a little while to get it ready again."

"All this, of course, is assuming that the thing is actually in there." Regan pointed out.

Evans sighed. "There is that."

As the late afternoon began giving way to evening on the following day Simms made his way into the hotel lobby in Atlantic City. He was directed to the ballroom towards the back of the first floor where he found Colonel Evans had set up his headquarters.

"Ah, DCI Simms." Evans said in greeting. "What's word from Dr. Nesbitt?"

"He told me earlier today he would have something to us by tomorrow morning. He and his staff were going to work through the night if necessary to get it to us." Simms answered.

Evans nodded. "Great. We should be ready here shortly."

"I noticed, from all the activities in the street, you have moved a lot of men and matériel in." Simms said.

Evans smiled. "Yes, we have. We have Army, National Guard and the local police all mobilized. Hell, we even have some firemen covering parts of the shoreline. We have almost everyone in place. I just hope we're in the right place."

"Sounds like you have the area pretty well covered." Simms observed.

"Hope so. It's the inland side that worries me the most. It's some pretty thick pine forest over there. Gonna be hard to track anything in there or move around if we need to." Evans said.

From somewhere outside the building they could hear a woman crying about something.

"What about planes?" Simms asked.

Evans shrugged. "We've got a few, but it's hard to see much through the forest cover or something swimming underwater from the sky. I'm afraid they won't be of much help."

"I thought I saw something large just offshore earlier." Simms said.

Evans gave Simms a sharp look. "Not another one?"

Simms hesitated. "Oh, no, not a creature. I think it was a battleship."

Evans smiled. "Oh, that. Yes, our friends in the Navy thought it would be prudent to have a little extra firepower on hand should we need it."

"Probably not a bad idea." Simms agreed.

A soldier appeared at Evans' side. He looked hesitant.

Evans glanced over at him. "Yes, what is it?"

"Uh, sir, there's a woman out here that insists on seeing who's ever in charge." The soldier said.

Evans started to say something. They could hear the woman crying out in the lobby. Evans waved a hand in resignation. "Let her in."

A moment later the soldier escorted an older woman into the ballroom.

"Yes ma'am?" Evans asked.

"Are you in charge here?" The woman asked between sniffles.

Evans gave a quick nod. "I am Colonel Evans." When he saw that didn't mean anything to the woman he continued. "I am in charge here."

"It's...it's my husband. He just disappeared." The woman said.

Evans glanced at Simms. He wasn't sure what to say. "Uh, well, I'm very sorry about that ma'am, but I'm sure he'll show up. Just give a description to one of my soldiers—-"

"No, sir. He's gone." The woman cut Evans off.

Evans sighed. "OK. I'm very sorry about your situation, but—-"

"He was there, in the boat and then he was gone." The woman said.

"As I was saying I'm very, wait, what did you say? He was in a boat?" Evans turned more to face the woman.

"Yes, sir. We were checking the pots early this morning. He goes out in the boat. I watch from the shore. One minute he was there pulling a pot and I only turned around for a moment, I swear, and he was gone. No husband. No boat. Just gone." The woman started crying again.

Evans studied the woman for a moment. "Is it possible the boat sank?"

The woman composed herself and looked at Evans like he was an idiot. "Sank? No. Pulling a pot in? No, sir. That boat was just fine. The water was calm and then when I looked back out they were gone. Boat and all. Just some waves and nothing."

"Waves?" Simms asked looking over at Evans.

Evans hesitated. "OK. Ma'am, can you show us where this happened?"

The woman sniffled and nodded her head.

Evans guided the woman over to a table covered with various maps. He shuffled a few around and slid a map in front of the woman. It was a map of the general area, but its primary focus was Atlantic City, Brigantine Island and the Absecon Swamp.

"Show me." Evans said.

The woman studied the map for just a moment and then pointed to a spot on the north edge of the swamp. "Right here."

Evans stared at it. "Are you sure?"

The woman nodded.

Evans glanced at Simms. "That's outside of the swamp. Is it heading back north?"

Simms stared at the map. "Not sure. But Dr. Reynolds, the paleontologist at the University in Washington, said the creature might have trouble finding where it wants to go because the shoreline would have changed a lot since it was last here."

The soldier escorted the woman back out of the ballroom while Simms and Evans both studied the map.

Simms reached out and pointed at the mouth of the Mullica River.

Evans nodded. "Just what I was thinking. It's a decent size river. A good place for it to move through. If only we knew for sure." He pounded a fist on to the table.

"How far up that river can we get in a Coast Guard cutter?" Simms asked.

"Don't know. Guess we'll find out." Evans yelled for an aide.

Evans glanced over at Simms. "In the meantime, we need to extend our pickets further out."

A soldier quickly appeared.

Evans turned to face the soldier. "I want men positioned on both sides of..." Evans glanced at the map and pointed, "the Mullica River for at least two miles inland."

The aide glanced at the map. "We're short on manpower still, sir. Should I pull men out of the city and reposition them up there?"

Evans frowned. "No. Can't do that. Can't leave the city undefended. If we are wrong and that thing shows up in Atlantic City there'll be hell to pay. No. Pull men out of that pine forest. Can't see a damned thing in there anyway."

"Yes sir." The soldier saluted and started to leave.

"Oh, and get Captain Jackson on the line." Evans glanced over at Simms. "Tell him we need a small cutter."

Simms nodded. A small boat on a river hunting a giant beast. Regan was going to love this, he thought.

17

"Holy crap it's foggy out here." Regan said. He clutched his gun staring out into the fog as it roiled up from the water all around them and knowing all the while his .45 would do little if anything against the beast should it rise up out of the water.

"It's soup. That's for sure." Evans agreed with a nod. The small Coast Guard cutter slowly approached the mouth of the Mullica River in the early gray dawn light.

"Ever shoot in fog like this before?" Nesbitt asked the sharpshooter next to him—the same guy that had taken down the first creature.

The sharpshooter shook his head a little. "Afraid not. We're gonna to have to be practically right on top of him to get any kind of shot in this stuff."

"Damn." Simms said looking around. "It doesn't get any better in there." Simms pointed towards the river, which they could only really tell was a river because shoreline was closing in towards them on either side.

"Gunner, stay alert up there." Evans called out to the sailor manning the machine gun mounted at the front of the cutter.

"Yes sir." The gunner replied. He was the forward most person on the cutter and he knew it. His head swiveled left and right staring as best he could into the milky slowly swirling fog. He gripped the machine gun tightly with both hands nervously.

"In this stuff he could be standing right over us before we even know it." Regan said. The tension clear in his voice.

"Steady." Evans said reassuringly.

There were a couple of soldiers on deck with them armed with rifles, but that was about all the men that could realistically fit on the forward deck. On the deck at Nesbitt's feet was the box that held the plutonium missile, waiting to be attached to the rifle the moment they spotted the creature. Both Nesbitt and the sharpshooter had radioactive protective garments on, but the others did not. There was not a great plan for protecting the others when the moment came for Nesbitt to retrieve the plutonium. The best they could agree on was that everyone would move as far back as possible and Nesbitt would try to shield them as best he could.

The cutter crept into the river. Everyone continued glancing in all directions hoping to catch a glimpse of some shadowy figure should it suddenly appear.

"14 feet." A voice called out from a window behind them in the bridge.

Evans turned to one of the soldiers on deck. "Tell him to keep it down. We need to listen as much as we can."

"Yes sir." The soldier scurried back to the bridge.

Minutes ticked past. There was only the faint sound of the cutter engine idling along and the quiet lap of water against the side of the boat. The river was very calm and peaceful.

Suddenly the boat rocked. The men staggered at the unexpected roll of the deck.

"What the hell...?" Regan said grabbing the rail.

"Did something hit us?" Simms asked.

Evans shook his head. "No. I think it was just a wave."

"A wave? What would...oh shit, never mind." Regan said.

"Yeah, well, at least we know it's here." Evans said quietly.

Nothing stirred in the fog. No movement. No sounds.

"Gunner look sharp up there." Evans said.

"Yes sir." No need to remind me, the gunner thought.

"10 feet." A voice quietly called out from the bridge window.

The sharpshooter leaned closer to Nesbitt. "I meant to ask you. Where am I targeting this beast?"

"Well, we're not exactly sure. To be honest, we're not even sure what this creature looks like." Nesbitt replied.

The sharpshooter scowled. "This isn't the same kind of beast as the other one?"

Nesbitt shook his head. "I don't think so. By the descriptions we've gotten, it seems like this creature is more serpentine."

"Serpentine?" The sharpshooter just looked at Nesbitt.

"He means it's more like a giant snake." Evans answered.

"Hmm, that's going to make the shot harder." The sharpshooter said, thinking about it.

"Can you do it?" Nesbitt asked.

The sharpshooter shrugged. "Might depend on where I have to hit it."

Nesbitt looked at Evans.

Evans sighed. "I guess I was thinking its hide would be easier to penetrate and it wouldn't matter."

"We've only got one shot." Nesbitt reminded him.

Nesbitt, Evans, Simms and Regan all exchanged looks.

"Damn." Evans said. He looked straight at the sharpshooter. "Think you could hit it in the mouth?"

The sharpshooter's eyes widened slightly. "Before or while he's eating me?"

Evans was about to rip into his subordinate for his answer when Simms spoke up.

"He's right. In this fog that thing would be right on top of him before he would get a clear view of its mouth."

Evans scowled at the sharpshooter. He turned to the two soldiers on deck. "You two."

"Yes sir." The soldiers answered.

"When he steps up for the shot," Evans pointed at the sharpshooter, "I want one of you on either side of him. You keep that beast off him while he takes that shot. Understood?"

"Yes sir." The soldiers answered with considerably less enthusiasm than before.

Evans drew his .45 out of his holster. He glanced at Simms who slid his gun out from under his coat as well. Silently it was agreed. They needed to give the sharpshooter his chance.

"8 feet." The voice from the bridge called again.

"We're shallowing fast." Simms said.

Evans nodded.

"What did Captain Jackson say the draft of this cutter was?" Simms asked.

"They lightened it up as much as they could. I think he said it was about 4 feet." Evans answered.

The rising sun in the East behind them helped a little with the fog. They gained some visual distance. At selected times they were able to see almost 20 feet in front of them. Despite the diminishing fog, it still felt very closed in.

Suddenly there was a scream and a gun shot from behind them. They all whirled around, but the scream had come from the back of the cutter which none of them could see from the front deck.

"What the hell?" Evans said.

"Something just got one of the sailors on the back deck." A voice called out from the bridge.

"All stop!" Evans shouted.

"Shit!"

They all turned back around towards the bow of the cutter where the sailor on the machine gun was desperately yanking the handles of the gun downward.

"What hell's he doing?" Regan asked.

"Oh, shit." Simms said. "He's trying to get the gun up." Simms pointed high above the front of the cutter. Much higher than any of them had been looking. There in the dim light of the fog, easily 30 or 40 feet above them was a reptilian head. The details of it were still blurred by the fog, but, later, the best description anyone could give was that it looked like a dragon.

A rumbling hoarse rasping sound hissed towards them, along with a hideous stench. Both soldiers began firing at the creature. The sailor at the machine gun fired, but he was clearly panicked and his aim was wild and inaccurate.

"Get the missile!" Evans yelled as he took a shot at the beast.

"You guys need to move back." Nesbitt called out.

"Just do it." Evans said over his shoulder.

Nesbitt and the sharpshooter both donned their hoods and gloves and knelt down next to the box with the plutonium. Nesbitt did his best to position himself between the box and the rest of the men.

With alarming speed the creature dove back underwater. The firing stopped and for a moment everyone stopped moving. The boat rocked from the wave caused by the creature's dive.

Evans glanced back at Nesbitt. "Keep going. Get it ready. He'll be back."

Nesbitt carefully pulled the missile out of the box and held it out to the sharpshooter so he could attach it to the end of his rifle. A sound like thunder accompanied the whole right side of the cutter lifting out of the water. The missile spun out of Nesbitt's grip and skittered across the deck towards the edge on the left side. It would have slid off into the river had not one of the soldiers fallen down on the deck. The missile skittered right into the chest of the soldier and rolled around in front of him.

As the boat righted itself the soldier, knowing full well what the missile contained, stared with wide eyes as it spun in circles in front of his chest. The sharpshooter scrambled across the deck and snatched the missile. It took him another few seconds to get it secured to the end of the rifle.

Everything got quiet again. Everyone was twisting and turning looking in every direction for the creature. There wasn't a sound except the waves lapping against the shore of the river.

"What about grenades, sir?" One of the soldiers asked.

Evans shook his head. "No. It might drive it off. We have it here now. We need to kill it."

The ship began backing slowly down the river.

"What the hell are they doing in there?" Evans asked spinning around to look at the bridge. "I said all stop!" He yelled at the window of the bridge.

A head poked out the window. "We are all stop."

Evans glanced at Simms. They exchanged a look.

"Damn. He's under the bow." Evans said. He tried to move forward, but the boat rocked slightly and he stumbled.

The backward movement slowed. And then it was there. The whole head. Just in front of the bow. The machine gunner yelled something and started firing, but, again, out of panic, it was apparent from the tracer rounds that his aim was too far right. The sound of the bullets whizzing past the creature's head caused it to lower its head down even with the deck and slide around to the left side of the cutter. The top of its head was just visible behind the railing moving down the left side.

As the beast's head rose above the railing the two soldiers began firing. The head dropped with frightening speed towards one of the soldiers. The soldier stumbled backwards, his gun now dropping out of his hands.

Evans, Simms and Regan were firing now as well. It was obvious, though, that the hide on this creature was pretty tough. Their bullets were having only a minor effect upon it.

The other soldier, in an act of great bravery, in order to distract the beast had lunged forward and took a mighty baseball swing at the head with the butt end of his rifle. It was valiant, but doomed to failure. If bullets weren't seriously harming the beast, then the butt of a rifle was not likely to bother it, but, as it turned out, it was exactly what was needed.

The creature saw the soldier lunging towards it and stopped going after the first soldier. It turned, mouth gaping, waiting for the second soldier to run right into its jaws. It was at that moment the sharpshooter slid across the deck to the left side and at nearly point blank range fired the missile into the creature's mouth.

With a garbled sound that seemed like something between a scream and a squawk, the creature lurched backwards. The beast lifted itself high up out of the water. It was now at 50 feet in the air and then it doubled back over itself slamming into the water. A great sheet of water washed over the deck of the cutter.

Something smacked into the boat on the left side of the bow. The boat rocked again and everyone had to grab something in order to not end up in the water. After a moment there was a wild thrashing in the water just ahead of the bow. At times portions of the creature were visible heaving out of the water and then disappearing again.

Finally, calmly the head of the creature rose up again. This time just forward of the right side of the bow. Everyone stood watching it. It hovered motionless, staring straight at them. Oddly, no one fired at it. The prehistoric beast and the men stared at each other. Then, slowly, the head and extended neck began leaning left, more and more until in sudden plunge the creature crashed into the water. Again soaking the men on deck. For another moment the upper part of the beast lay on the surface before slowly sinking quietly into the dark waters of the Mullica River.

18

"And that was the last we saw of it." Simms said, finishing his story.

Marcus sat at the head of the table. He stared down at an array of papers spread out in front of him.

"What is the level of confidence that this second creature is dead?" Marcus asked. His question wasn't directed at anyone in particular, although his eyes did go to Colonel Evans.

"We dragged the Mullica River the following day. That's as soon as we could get the equipment in there. We didn't come up with anything. If I had to bet on it, I'd bet that one is as dead as the first one." Evans said.

"I agree." Nesbitt added. "The marksman's shot was point blank into the throat of that creature. I cannot imagine any living thing could have survived that plutonium shot."

Lee Hunter sat next to Professor Nesbitt and smiled over at him.

Again Marcus was quiet for a moment. "So, we do not have any sample from the second creature?"

"No sir." Simms answered.

"I would have liked to get a sample of that beast as well." Marcus said this, but obviously more to himself.

"What did the analysis of the blood sample from the first creature show?" Evans asked.

Marcus shook his head slightly. "Not much. We know that it is deadly. What we do not know is if it can easily be passed from person to person. We know it is something we have never seen before."

"The word from New York is that those individuals with significant exposure all died. Those with less exposure had a 50% mortality. All those affected by the disease have either died or are recovered so there is currently no one showing any further signs of it." Simms reported.

"That was my primary concern with the disease. The high mortality rate. If it turned out to be highly contagious then we would be looking at a serious pandemic." Marcus said.

"Well, thankfully, both creatures are dead and no more have shown up." Evans said. "Hopefully, we are done with the damned things. And, with them gone, so is the disease."

Simms glanced over at Marcus. Only the OSO agents, that knew that Marcus had a portion of the sample frozen and locked away in a special vault. If such a disease reappeared they would need something from which to work on a vaccine.

"Assuming then that this second creature is in fact dead, we need to keep a watch out for its carcass. If it too carried the disease then its remains might still be a threat." Marcus said.

Evans nodded. "I thought of that when we couldn't dredge the body up. I talked to the Coast Guard and they are going to keep watch of the shoreline. It's quite possible, though, the body may have been carried out of the river by the current and then on out to sea on the tide."

"Agreed." Marcus nodded. "I want to thank all of you for your hard work on this."

"Well," Evans said with a smile and slap of his hand on the table, "maybe we can get on to discussing happier topics. Like when the two of you are getting married." He looked over at Nesbitt and Lee Hunter.

Nesbitt and Lee looked at each other and smiled, but didn't answer Evans.

From the case files of the
Office of Scientific Operations:

Public Release #1B

File #157

1954

Commonly referred to by the
public as "Them"

1

Marcus Edmonds, Director of the OSO, a stocky well dressed man in his fifties, sat at his desk and stared at the folder laying open on it. He wasn't sure what to make of it. Was it something the OSO needed to investigate or was it just an odd sounding missing person's case? Marcus tried to be careful about how he allocated OSO resources. President Eisenhower had never given Marcus any sense that the OSO did not remain an important part of the U.S. intelligence community. Still, Marcus did not like the idea of sending his agents out on wild goose chases.

Marcus flipped a page laying on the desk without really looking at it. He had already been through the file twice. He might have quickly dismissed this information had it not been sent over from Director Connors at the FBI. Marcus had known Connors for some years and felt he was a man of sound judgment and instincts. If Connors felt like there might be something here worth investigating, then Marcus felt like he should at least consider it as well.

He walked through what was currently known. FBI agent Ellinson on vacation in New Mexico has disappeared. The FBI sent an agent by the name of Robert Graham to investigate. Graham and a Sgt Ben Peterson of the New Mexico State Police, one of the officers that reported the disappearance, have found the travel trailer of Ellinson. The trailer was badly damaged. The current assessment of what caused the damage to the trailer is unknown. No sign of Ellinson or his family was found.

In addition, a small grocery store in the general vicinity of the Ellinson's trailer was also heavily damaged. Again, the cause of the damage was unknown, but the grocer was found dead at the scene. The cause of his death was unclear, but a large amount of formic acid was found in his body. That was a very odd fact. Director Connors has sent a couple of scientists from the Department of Agriculture to New Mexico to assist in the investigation. Marcus was unclear as to why scientists from the Department of Agriculture were chosen, but those were the current facts of the case.

The question now was what was Marcus going to do, if anything. Many cases came across his desk and, as Director, it was his responsibility to sift through them and determine which ones were genuine threats or potential threats to the safety of the United States. Often, such as this case, it was complicated by having only minimal facts to base that decision upon. It usually came down to Marcus' instincts.

Marcus reached out and flipped on the intercom to his secretary Jennifer.

"Jennifer?"

"Yes, Mr. Edmonds?" Jennifer replied.

"Will you ask Elliot to join me in my office?" Marcus asked. Elliot Simms was the senior investigator on the OSO staff. He was a smart, level-headed guy and Marcus could see, at some point in the future, Elliot moving into the Director's position.

"Yes sir." Jennifer replied.

District Chief Investigator Elliot Simms walked into his boss' office.

"You wanted to see me, sir?" Simms asked. He was of medium build, dark brown hair and, as usual, had a serious look to him.

"Have a seat Elliot." Marcus slid the folder over to Elliot who flipped through the handful of pages in it and looked up at Marcus.

"What do you think?" Marcus asked.

"Not a lot here." Simms replied.

Marcus nodded. "Agreed."

"Seems odd for an FBI agent to just disappear, along with his entire family." Simms commented.

"I agree. I asked Director Connors over at the FBI about Ellinson. Seems like he was a reliable and solid agent. No reason to think he might have...had some issue or become unstable." Marcus said.

"The description of the damage to the trailer is...strange." Simms said, staring at the pages in front of him.

Marcus nodded again. "That too, caught my eye."

"And it's assumed that the attack on the small grocery store is connected to the incident with the trailer?" Simms asked.

"It is." Marcus said.

"So, are you thinking we should take a look?" Simms asked.

Marcus sighed. "I am inclined to send you and DI Regan down to New Mexico, just to take a closer look. It may be nothing."

"We can fly down there and evaluate the situation, sir." Simms said.

"Honestly, if DI Wayne and DI Wyatt were available I would probably assign something like this to them, but they are still down in South America interviewing people there." Marcus said.

"That 'Gillman' thing?" Simms asked.

Marcus nodded. "Yes. Still trying to determine if that was a real thing. If that creature from..."

"I think they referred to it as the 'Black Lagoon.'" Simms volunteered.

"Right. If that thing actually existed. Anyway, they probably won't return until the end of the week." Marcus said.

Simms reached out and picked up the folder. "I will bring DI Regan up to speed and we will head out to New Mexico."

"I will have Jennifer make the arrangements." Marcus said with a quick nod.

Simms stood up and then hesitated. "Sir?"

"Yes?" Marcus looked up at Simms.

"The high level of formic acid in the dead grocer...?" Simms shook his head slightly.

Marcus frowned. "I don't know what to make of that either. Another minor mystery to solve."

Simms nodded. "Guess so."

2

"It's pretty empty out here." District Investigator "Robbie" Regan said from the back seat as the New Mexico State Trooper drove them out to the sight of the trailer where Ellinson and his family disappeared. Regan's sandy blonde hair and bright features gave him a cheery look.

"Not too many people out here." The Trooper agreed.

Simms sat in the front seat staring out at the surrounding desert. A light breeze was blowing stirring some dust along the way. He understood why the government had put the development of it's atomic weapons program in places like this. They couldn't be much more than twenty miles from Alamogordo, where the first atomic bombs were tested.

They could see even as the dust kicked up some in the early afternoon light that there was something just a little ways up on the right. As they pulled up to a stop at the place it looked more or less like a tranquil place for a camping site.

They got out of the car.

"Looks peaceful enough." Simms said.

"It's over here." The Trooper said, leading them around, past the station wagon and to the opposite side of the travel trailer.

"Holy shit." Regan said as they stopped to stare at the side of the trailer. "What hit that thing?"

Simms shook his head. "Don't know, but..." He walked forward, closer to the trailer. "...it looks like the metal side was torn open."

The metal that comprised the wall of the front side of the trailer was sticking out in jagged shreds. There had been a door there and above it a shade canopy. There were only remnants of the door remaining and the canopy had been shredded. Some camp furniture and other assorted items that had been sitting just outside the trailer were scattered all about.

Regan wandered around the sight. "Do they get tornadoes out here?"

Simms had poked his head into the trailer. "Tornadoes aren't this precise."

"This doesn't look all that precise." Regan said as he slowly twirled around.

Simms joined Regan among the debris. "Whatever hit this spot was targeting just this trailer. Nothing else seemed to be disturbed. If it had been wind that did this you'd expect these big cactus trees—-"

"Joshua Trees." The Trooper said.

"Ah, OK, Joshua Trees. You'd think they would show at least a little beating too, but they look fine." Simms said. "In addition, look at some of the markings on the side of the trailer."

"You mean those big scratches?" Regan asked pointing at the trailer.

"Yeah. There's some more like it inside." Simms answered.

Regan wandered around to the back of the trailer.

"You're local here. Seen anything like this before?" Simms asked the Trooper.

The Trooper shook his head. "Never. It's a new one on me. We got mountain lions, coyotes, snakes and sandstorms, but none of those do anything like this."

Simms nodded. "Yeah. This is strange." He stood looking around.

"Hey, Elliot!" Regan called from the back of the trailer.

Simms circled around the trailer. He was about to ask Regan what he wanted as he walked up to him when a sound in the distance drew his attention. He turned and scanned the horizon.

"You hear that?" Regan asked.

Simms just nodded.

"It's some kind of weird chirping or ringing. Can't see anything, though." Regan said, also looking all around.

"We're kind of in a low spot here." Simms said. He started moving further out away from the trailer and the road. Regan followed. They walked up a small rise. The afternoon sun was intensely bright, but the dust blowing in the wind made it seem dim.

"There! What's that?" Regan said pointing into the distance.

Simms followed Regan's direction. At first he didn't see anything and then what he thought was a shadow that seemed to move. It was difficult to determine it's size and impossible to tell what it was. They watched it for another moment before it disappeared below another sandy rise. The sound diminished and was gone.

"What do you think?" Regan asked.

Simms slowly shook his head. "Don't know."

"Should we go take a look?" Regan was trying to catch sight of it again.

"No. It's too hard to see in all this blowing sand. We'd have a hard time finding it. Might not be anything more than a trick of the swirling dust." Simms said.

Regan glanced over at Simms. "I don't think that was any trick. I think something was there."

With a shrug, Simms walked back down the sandy rise. They climbed back into the car and the Trooper drove them on to the grocery store.

They stood outside the large hole in the wooden wall of the store.

"Wow. Somebody sure wanted to get into this place." Regan said

Simms nodded. "Sure looks like it. Seems like it would have been a whole lot easier to just smash the front window than to tear through the wall."

"Yeah." Regan said.

"Have the Forensics people already been through here?" Simms asked.

"Yes, sir." The Trooper answered.

Simms stepped over what remained of the wall and into the store. Regan and the Trooper followed him in. The Trooper stood just inside the wall. Simms and Regan slowly walked around the mess. There were shelves smashed, barrels dumped, glass items broken and dry goods scattered everywhere.

"Where was the body found?" Simms asked.

The Trooper pointed towards the right side of the store. "Over there. In the cellar. There's a door in the floor."

Simms nodded. "I see it." He walked over and glanced down through the two adjoining sections of floor that pulled on hinges to reveal a storage area underneath the store. Regan carefully made his way through the mess to stand next to Simms and stare down at the opening.

"If you were going to make a mess like this, why bother to try to hide the body?" Regan asked.

"I agree. One of these doors was even left open." Simms said.

"You think the killer wanted us to find the body?" Regan asked.

"I don't know. Doesn't make sense. With all of this," Simms waved at the room around them, "how could we not find the body?"

"Yeah." Regan replied.

Simms turned to the Trooper. "This is the place your fellow Trooper disappeared isn't it?"

"Yes, sir. He was waiting for the Forensic people to show up. Nobody has seen him since. They found his gun on the ground outside." The Trooper answered.

"Any shots fired?" Simms asked.

The Trooper nodded. "Five out of six bullets."

"Five shots and he didn't hit anything?" Regan asked.

The Trooper shrugged. "Yeah. Doesn't make sense. He was a good shot."

The breeze blew and some of the boards hanging around the edge of where the wall had been torn out creaked. There was another sound carried by the wind. It was a chirping ringing sound.

Simms and Regan looked at one another. They quickly moved back to opening in the wall and stepped outside. The Trooper followed them around to the side of the building. Only the Trooper had his gun drawn. They stood trying to see something. The Trooper clicked on his flashlight in an attempt to cut through the blowing sand and swung it around. Nothing. The sound continued for another minute and then faded.

Simms turned to the Trooper. "Ever hear anything like that before?"

The Trooper shook his head. "No, sir. Never. No idea what that was."

Simms glanced at Regan who shook his head. They walked back to the car. The Trooper started the car, did a U-turn and headed back towards town. They rode in silence for a little while

"Well, this is weird." Regan finally said.

Simms nodded. "It is."

"Probably not as weird as what Wayne and Wyatt are looking into." Regan commented.

Simms shrugged. "Don't know."

"You think that creature thing really existed?" Regan asked.

"I don't know. That's why they went down there. To find out." Simms answered.

"Well, they say it's dead now, so we'll probably never know." Regan said.

"You guys talking about that Gillman?" The Trooper asked.

"Yeah." Regan replied.

"I read about that. Man, there is a lot of crazy stuff going on these days." The Trooper said.

Simms and Regan glanced at each other.

"Does seem that way." Simms said quietly.

3

The following morning found everyone crowded into an office at the State Police station. Simms and Regan introduced themselves to both of the scientists from the Department of Agriculture, Dr. Harold Medford and his daughter, Dr. Pat Medford. Also present were Sgt Ben Peterson, the New Mexico State Trooper that had first found the Ellinson's trailer and FBI Agent Robert Graham—-the man sent out by Director Connors.

"Ants?" Regan asked.

"Yes. Ants." Dr. Medford said.

"Big ants?" Regan asked again.

"Yes, DI Regan, these are ants. About six, maybe seven feet in length." Graham, the FBI agent, replied.

"Couldn't we just spray the area and kill them off?" Simms asked.

"No, no, we must find the nest." Dr. Medford said.

"The nest?" Simms asked glancing around at the gathering.

"Yes, the nest. We must get rid of...do we really need to go through this again? Time is short. Who are you two gentlemen again?" Dr. Medford said. He was a short slightly round man in his sixties. It was apparent that he was excitable and tended to be focused on whatever was his current task.

"Dad, please." Pat Medford said.

"These men are from the OSO." Graham said.

"The what?" Dr. Medford asked.

"The Office of Scientific Operations." Simms answered.

"Oh." Dr. Medford hesitated. "I think I have heard of you guys. OK, well, gentlemen we have to find the nest and make sure we eliminate the queen. Otherwise, well, we will be battling these ants for who knows how long."

"So, as I understand it, you want to take a couple of helicopters from the air base here and scout the surrounding area for the nest?" Simms asked.

"Yes, yes. And the sooner the better." Dr. Medford replied.

Simms turned to look at Sgt Peterson. "Are there more homesteads in this general area? Places that have not been checked on as yet?"

Peterson nodded. "Yeah. There's a few."

"I think it would be prudent to check on them as well. Could I get a list of those places?" Simms asked.

"Sure thing." Peterson answered. "We don't really have the manpower at the moment, though, to give you an armed escort."

"That's OK. We'll bring along a couple of soldiers from the air base with us." Simms said.

"Oh, and I don't know what kind of weapons you may have brought along with you, but I recommend you stock up on some heavier guns while you're at the air base. In case you encounter any ants. Hand guns had minimal effect upon them." Graham suggested.

Simms gave a nod. "We'll do that. Thanks."

At the air base Simms and Regan were stopped at the gate.

"What's the problem?" Simms asked the guard at the gate.

"I'm sorry sir, but I have not been notified of your arrival." The soldier stared back at Simms. He seemed to be unsure of whether he was doing the right thing or not. Just beyond the gate a jeep pulled up. An officer climbed out and walked up to them. The soldier turned and saluted.

"Major Kibbee, these men..." The soldier started.

"I'll handle this." Major Kibbee told the guard. He turned back to Simms and spoke to him through the window of their car.

"I'm Major Kibbee. General O'Brien sends his regards. He says we are to extend you every courtesy and provide you with any assistance you might require." Kibbee said, shaking Simms' hand.

"Thank you, Major Kibbee." Simms replied.

"I heard the OSO had a hand in that business with those big reptiles in New York and New Jersey. Is that true?" Kibbee said.

"Oh, yeah." Regan answered from the passenger seat. "We had ringside seats for that."

Simms glanced at Regan and then back to Kibbee. "We did assist the military in that operation. Were you there?"

Kibbee shook his head. "No. I was stationed at West Point and transferred out here several months before all that took place."

"So any suggestions on what weapons we should take for these ants?" Simms asked.

Kibbee thought for a minute. "Well, I haven't seen these things yet. I guess rifles would be a start. Oh, you know, in the war, in the infantry we had a saying, 'When in doubt, use a bazooka'. Course we saw our fair share of panzers."

"What unit were you in?" Simms asked.

"The First." Kibbee answered.

"The Big Red One." Simms nodded with respect.

"The Bloody First." Kibbee smiled. "And you?"

"Army Intelligence." Simms replied.

Kibbee gave a knowing nod. "Of course. Anyway, I would throw in a bazooka."

"For an ant?" Regan asked.

"A seven foot ant." Simms said.

"Well, if it'll stop a tank it outta stop an ant." Kibbee pointed out.

Regan nodded in agreement. "OK, I can buy that."

Kibbee hesitated. "Maybe a flamethrower. You know, just for good measure."

"That should be enough." Simms said.

"Follow me. We'll find you a couple of volunteers and get you guys loaded up." Kibbee said.

"OK." Simms said and slipped the car into gear.

4

"So which way?" Regan said looking at Simms.

Simms sighed. "I don't know." He gave an inquisitive look to Brooks and Conley, the two soldiers sitting in the back seat. They glanced at each other and slowly shook their heads at Simms.

They had already been to two small homesteads. The first showed some of the same damage that the trailer and the grocery store had sustained. There were no people anywhere to be found at that place. There were a couple of blood stains. One in the sandy yard and one just inside a window alongside the house where the bulk of the damage had occurred. The place was quiet and no sign of the people that had lived there could be found.

At the second place there was no sign of anything. Another small shack sitting among cactus, Joshua Trees and piles of sand. Again, they didn't find any people, but there was no sign of any kind of violence there. They agreed that, hopefully, the people had fled before the ants got them.

Now they sat at an intersection where a side road dumped into the road they were on. They were having trouble interpreting the directions on where the last homestead was.

"Well, I think, if we keep going this way," Regan pointed at the map indicating further along the road they had been driving along, "we are going to end up way over here somewhere. I think that's too far out. The directions don't sound like this place was way the hell out there."

Simms glanced up the road they were on and then over at the side road. "Alright. What the hell." He started the car up again and turned down the side road.

This side road was rougher than the road they had been on and the car bounced around. It added to a certain apprehension they all felt that this was not the direction they should be going in. Fortunately, after only a short bumpy distance down the road they spotted another small house. Simms pulled the car up in front of the house and stopped. They all got out.

"Hello!" Regan yelled.

Simms glanced down at the paper Sgt Peterson had provided them. "Mr. Hastings?" Simms called out.

Nothing. No sound.

Simms turned back towards the soldiers. "Spread out and take a look around."

With a nod the two soldiers, each carrying a rifle moved off towards the right side of the house. Simms, without saying anything, waved at Regan to follow him and they started slowly around the left side of the house.

Half way along the left side lay some broken boards. Simms and Regan walked over to them. When they reached the boards they realized this was the remains of a door to a root cellar. It was the width of a normal door frame. The wood that had comprised the door were still in place, but broken and pointing in various directions.

"Something wrecked this." Regan said.

"Yeah." Simms agreed and then stopped. "Wait. Did you hear something?"

They stood there in silence for a moment and then they heard it. It was a muffled sound. They both looked down at the broken root cellar door.

Simms knelt down next to the shattered door. "Hello?"

More muffled sounds.

Simms waved at Regan and they began pulling at the boards. After another minute they had cleared about half the door out of the way.

"Is anyone down there?" Regan called.

"Yeah. We're here." It was a hoarse and raspy voice.

"Hang on. We'll get you out." Simms yelled down to them.

"No." The voice replied.

"What?" Regan said.

"We're going to get you out." Simms repeated, thinking the person didn't hear him clearly the first time.

"No." The voice said again. "Run!"

Simms and Regan looked at each other. A chirping sound came from somewhere behind them. They whirled around and, at the same moment, they heard rifle shots coming from the far side of the house.

Over a small sandy rise thirty feet away something black was moving rapidly towards them. Simms pulled out his .45 and started shooting. Regan whipped the rifle he was carrying around and began firing as well. After the first few shots the ant seemed to slow down and hesitate.

"Where's your rifle?" Regan asked.

"In the car." Simms said.

"They said hand guns won't work." Regan said.

"Doesn't seem like the rifle is doing much either. Let's get back to the car and get the bazooka." Simms called out.

Regan waved at the cellar door. "What about whoever is in there?"

"I don't think the ants can fit down there. Besides, I think they will follow us. We can lure them away." Simms said firing off a couple more shots.

"Bait. Wonderful. I just love our plans." Regan said. He took another shot at the ant as it now decided to edge closer to them.

More shots came from the other side of the house along with a couple of shouts. Neither Simms nor Regan could make out what was being shouted, but somehow they felt like it was meant for them.

They made it past the corner of the house and scrambled back to the car. The two soldiers, Brooks and Conley, were already back to the car and had the trunk open.

"Grab the bazooka!" Simms yelled to the soldiers as he and Regan drew near.

Conley pulled the bazooka out while Brooks grabbed a couple of shells. The two soldiers moved forward again towards the right corner of the house.

"No. Left." Simms shouted to them and pointed. "There's people trapped over there."

Conley glanced back and nodded. Brooks followed.

Simms grabbed his rifle and went to support the two soldiers. Regan circled around to the back of the car.

At the corner of the house Conley had stopped and dropped to one knee. Brooks slid the shell into the bazooka and tapped Conley on the shoulder. A second later Conley fired.

Simms came up to them just in time to watch the bazooka shell zipped harmlessly by the ant. Simms started firing at the ant while Brooks quickly loaded another shell.

Conley fired again hitting the ground right between the front and middle left legs of the ant. The explosion blew most of both of those legs off. The ant stopped. Conley stood up and all three men stood watching the ant. It started wiggling and they assumed it was in some kind of death throes.

Suddenly the remaining legs of the ant gained some leverage and it lunged forward. It's pincers grabbed Conley while it's head knocked both Brooks and Simms backwards. With one crunching sound and a scream from Conley, he was dead.

Simms struggled to grab his rifle and then started firing again at the side of the ant. Brooks scrambled on all fours further along the front of the house to get away.

Then a roaring sound filled the air and fire engulfed the head of the ant. Regan, standing directly in front of the ant, waved the flamethrower at it. A moment later the head of the ant slumped to the ground and it was, without a doubt this time, dead.

Simms scrambled to his feet and moved around the dead ant. He walked over to the door of the root cellar.

"Are you people OK in there?" Simms called down through the wrecked door.

"We're alive." A woman's voice replied.

"Well, we'll have you—-" Suddenly there was a chirping noise coming from the back corner of the house. Simms looked up to see an ant moving quickly around from the back of the house towards him. He glanced back towards the front of the house and the still burning ant. There was no one in sight. In particular, DI Regan and his flamethrower.

Simms fired once with the rifle and, recognizing that the rifle alone was not going to stop the ant, dove through the partially destroyed door to the root cellar. He rolled roughly down the wooden steps and landed flat on his back on the cool dirt floor.

"DCI Simms with the OSO." Simms said glancing at the wide eyed man and woman and their two children huddled in a corner of the cellar.

Simms got up on his knees and swung around to face the door just as the ant began trying to fit it's pincers through the broken door. He fired twice, but his only real targets were the pincers and it was like shooting at sharp blades of steel. The only thing that kept the ant from getting in and killing them all was the fact that it's head couldn't quite fit through the doorway. That's what had kept this family alive up to this point, but if the ants began tearing the house over their heads away, which they were obviously fully capable of doing, they would be killed.

Finally there was roar and Simms could glimpse at least part of the ant going up in flame. A whiff of fuel and smoke smell swirled into the cellar and everyone started coughing. The smell passed, but only to be replaced with a nasty acrid smell of what Simms decided was the distinct odor of cooked ant.

It took Regan and Brooks a couple of minutes to pull the charred ant away from the door so Simms and the trapped family could climb out.

"Oh thank you, thank you." Mrs. Hastings said as she emerged.

"Are they all dead?" Mr. Hastings asked.

Simms shook his head. "Not all of them. Just these two. We'd better get out of here now before more come."

Everyone squeezed into the car as best they could. They had no choice except to leave Conley's body where it was for now. Brooks volunteered to sit in the open trunk so the Hastings could all fit in the back seat. Simms got the car going and they pulled out on to the small side road.

"Sir?" Mr. Hastings said from the back seat.

"Yes?" Simms replied as he tried to drive as fast as he could down the rugged road without injuring anyone in the car or tossing Brooks out of the trunk in the back.

"What's an OSO?"

5

Simms and Regan left the Hastings family in the main office area of the State Police station. They walked into the office where the principal people involved in dealing with the ants, including General O'Brien and Major Kibbee, had already been engaged in a meeting.

It took a little while for Simms to explain what they found at the outlying homesteads.

"Ah, well, much as I would expect." Dr. Medford said nodding.

"Dr. Medford was showing us what a typical ant colony would look like." Kibbee waved a hand towards a drawing that had been hung up on the wall. Simms and Regan walked over to the drawing and stared at it.

"OK. Do we know where their colony is?" Simms asked.

Kibbee nodded. "Yes. We identified it from the air this afternoon."

"Good." Simms said. "So, what's the plan? Bomb the nest?"

Dr. Medford sighed. "Always with the bombs."

Pat laughed. "No, DCI Simms. We're going to catch the ants in their nest in the hottest part of the day and use gas to kill them off."

"Won't they just run out some other hole?" Regan asked.

"I'm going to seal off every hole we can find within a 10 mile radius. We'll use explosives to collapse the holes. That should keep them inside long enough for the gas to kill them off." General O'Brien explained.

"OK, what can we do to help?" Simms asked.

"I was thinking you could take charge of getting those other holes closed off." O'Brien said.

Simms nodded. "OK. We can do that. Should we be trying to do that tonight?"

"No, Dr. Medford says the ants are most active at night when it is cooler. It's safer if we operate in the daylight hours and the holes will be easier to spot during the day anyway." Kibbee answered.

"Got it." Simms hesitated for a moment. "Once the gas dissipates, how will we know if we got all the ants?"

"We have to go in." Dr. Medford said.

"In?" Regan asked.

"Yes, into the nest. We have to make sure no other queen ants have escaped." Dr. Medford explained.

"Walking around in a small tunnel looking for killer ants? Wonderful." Regan said.

"Ah, my dear boy," Dr. Medford said patting Regan on the shoulder, "they'll most likely be all dead from the gas. Not a thing to worry about."

"It's the 'most likely' part that worries me." Regan replied.

"Dr. Medford," Simms said, "if the ants don't like to be out in the heat of the day, why have we encountered several out in the daylight?" Simms asked.

"You know, I have been pondering that myself." Dr. Medford replied. "I believe that, while these are essentially a known species of ant whose behaviors we are quite familiar with, these giants are clearly a variation of the species. Perhaps their behavior does not exactly match those of their tiny brethren."

"So, it's possible that beyond just size these ants may exhibit some characteristics that you have never seen before?" Simms asked.

Dr. Medford thought for a moment. "You know, I hadn't really thought about to what extent that could be true. That is very concerning. Very concerning, indeed." Dr. Medford slowly walked away, now deep in thought.

Pat sighed and smiled as she walked past Simms. "Thanks. Now he'll be up all night wanting to discuss that."

"Sorry." Simms said.

6

They had been flying around in the helicopter now for a while without spotting any other holes into the ant nest. The morning air was cool outside and Dr. Medford and forewarned them that the cool morning meant that the ants might still be fairly active until the sun finally drove them back underground for the day.

"Hey, there's one." Regan said pointing.

Simms leaned over to try to see out the left side of the helicopter.

"A hole?" Simms asked.

"No. An ant." Regan answered.

"Well, we're looking for the holes." Simms said sitting back.

"I know, but maybe we could follow the ant back to the hole." Regan suggested.

"How do you know it's going back to the hole and not further away?" Simms asked.

Regan thought for a moment. "I don't know, but it looks tired so I think it must be headed back to the nest."

"And you know what a tired ant looks like?" Simms said staring out his side of the helicopter.

Regan shrugged, though Simms wasn't looking at him to see it. "Well, it's mid-morning now anyway. I thought they all went back into the nest before it got hot." Regan said.

"Now that makes sense. I guess it's worth a try." Simms leaned forward and gave the pilot instructions to move in the direction the ant was headed, but not to lose sight of the ant.

The helicopter moved faster than the ant so they ended up circling out in front of the ant covering a wide range of ground that the ant could potentially end up moving towards. Finally Simms spotted something and the helicopter veered off to the right.

As they flew over the spot they could see it was clearly an ant hole. Moving a short distance away the pilot set the helicopter down, but kept the engine idling in case they needed to lift off quickly.

Simms, Regan and a soldier, whose specialty was demolitions, jumped out. Regan and the soldier, Corporal Cramer, each held a rope handle of the wooden crate that held dynamite. They carried the crate with them as they approached the ant hole. Simms kept an eye out for ants while wielding a machine gun.

They peeked into the hole, but didn't see any ants. Corporal Cramer began working at the edge of the hole preparing the dynamite for detonation.

"Should we wait for that other ant to get here and go back down into the hole?" Regan asked.

Simms shook his head. "No. We don't know for sure it was heading directly back here. We could be sitting here all day waiting for it."

At Corporal Cramer's request Regan slid over to where Cramer was kneeling by the crate and lent him a hand. Simms rotated slowly around and looked out past the helicopter. He wasn't sure if the sound of helicopter idling would deter an ant or attract one, but didn't want an ant sneaking up on the pilot if they found the sound alluring in some way.

Regan looked up from his work with Cramer. He pointed over Simms' shoulder beyond the hole.

"Our friend is here." Regan said.

Simms spun around. The ant they had followed was lumbering along towards the hole and the three of them. Simms opened fire with the machine gun. Some of the bullets struck home and some seemed to glance off the armored shell of the ant. It was enough, though, to slow the ant down.

The ant finally reached the far side of the hole from the three men. Simms' gun ran out of ammo. The ant was still moving, but very slowly now. Simms glanced down at Regan who pulled his .45 out and took aim. Before Regan could fire a shot the ant slumped to the ground and stopped moving.

"Well, that was close." Regan said.

"Yeah." Simms agreed. "And I am all out of ammo. You better hurry it up."

Regan glanced over at Cramer.

Cramer nodded. "We're set." He stood up and started spooling wire out as they all backed towards the helicopter. At the helicopter, Cramer cut the wires and transferred them to a detonator.

"Here comes another." Regan said, pointing towards the hole. The head of an ant appeared above the rim of the hole.

"Cover your ears." Cramer shouted over the sound of the helicopter's idling motor. Simms and Regan covered their ears and the blast shook the ground all around them. Dust flew in all directions from the hole. Through the dust something big and black came hurtling towards them. Simms pulled out his .45 and, along with Regan, took aim at the black thing.

Before any shots were fired, the dust cleared some and the black thing landed about fifteen feet to their left. It was the head of the ant in the hole.

"Whoa." Regan said looking over at the ant's head. He walked over to it. He stared at the pincers. Simms walked over and joined him. Suddenly the pincers on either side snapped shut about a foot in front of Simms and Regan. They jumped back.

"Shit." Regan said.

"Yeah." Simms said, regaining his balance. "Better remember that next time."

They walked over to where the hole had been. It was just a crater full of sand now. Nothing said the ants couldn't just dig their way back out, but when the gas hit the tunnels below, the ants weren't going to be escaping from here in a hurry. They'd be dead before they could clear this hole out again.

Simms, Regan and Cramer climbed back into the helicopter. Back up in the air they started circling out away from the hole they had just destroyed.

It took them only a few minutes more flying around to spot another one. They landed and repeated the process of moving the explosives to the hole. Simms had reloaded the machine gun and this time carried extra ammo with him.

Regan helped Cramer again with the dynamite while Simms watched for ants. At one point Simms thought he heard an ant and they sat listening, but no ants appeared.

They finished setting the explosives and retreated back to the helicopter. They covered their ears and Cramer set off the explosives. With another boom another hole was sealed off. They climbed back into the helicopter and were off again.

They circled some more, but did not spot another hole. They decided to make one last circle further out just to be certain. If any holes were left open the ants would have a chance to escape the cyanide gas and the threat would continue. Time, though, was not on their side. They knew the operation at the hole Pat had discovered would start soon and the hole closing needed to be completed by then.

They were just starting to turn back towards the only remaining open hole where everyone else was when Regan grabbed Simms' shoulder.

"What's that?" Regan asked pointing at something nestled into a clump of the some of the scraggly desert bushes.

Simms stared at it through his binoculars. "Not sure." Simms tapped on the shoulder of the pilot and pointed to the bushes. The helicopter swung around and they landed not far from the spot.

Simms and Regan walked up to the bushes. They could see that one section of bushes had been cleared away and they spotted the hole once they were close enough. Simms turned and signaled to Cramer to bring the explosives.

Once again Regan and Cramer worked on the explosives while Simms checked the hole and then patrolled around the area watching for ants.

"Hey." Regan called to Simms and waved for him to come back to the hole.

Simms walked back over the hole.

Regan pointed into the hole. "You hear something?"

Simms leaned closer. "Yeah. I think I hear something. Can't tell what it is though."

"Well, it's not a beautiful blonde." Regan said.

Simms gave Regan a look. "OK, so it's probably an ant. Let's hurry it up."

At that moment, the edge of the hole crumbled slightly and, with a yell, Cramer slid down into the hole. He fell about ten feet down and landed with a thump.

"Shit." Simms said dropping to a knee. "Cramer?"

"I'm here." Cramer said. "I'm OK. It's all sand down here."

Simms looked over at Regan. "Go get a rope."

Regan took off towards the helicopter.

"Hang in there. We're getting a rope." Simms called down to Cramer.

"Sir? I hear something." Cramer said.

"What do you hear?" Simms asked.

"Not sure, but it's getting closer." Cramer replied.

"Damn. Here." Simms dropped the machine gun down to Cramer. Simms stood up and yelled to Regan to bring the flamethrower too.

"What the hell?" Cramer could be heard saying.

"What is it?" Simms asked.

"The gun won't cock. It's jammed. I think it got sand in it." Cramer said, there was an edge of panic in his voice.

"Shit." Simms said as Regan was returning to the hole.

"Tie that rope around a couple of those bushes and use your body to anchor it. And give me that flamethrower." Simms said moving fast to grab the flamethrower.

"Look out." Simms called down to Cramer. "I'm coming down."

Simms didn't put the flamethrower on. He held the flamethrower by the straps and slid over the edge of the hole. He dropped down right next to Cramer hitting him in the shoulder with the tank of the flamethrower.

"Sorry." Simms apologized.

"I'm fine." Cramer said. "I'm so happy to see that flamethrower I would've caught it with my teeth."

The rope dropped down landing on Simms' head. He brushed if off.

"Get going." Simms waved at the rope while looking at Cramer.

"Are you—-oh shit." Cramer said snatching at the rope and staring down the tunnel.

From the tunnel that sloped down and to the left from the landing spot at the bottom of the hole the head of an ant could been seen approaching.

Simms spun around to see the ant. "Go. It's going to get hot down here real quick." He turned the valve of the flamethrower sitting on the ground next to him. He swung the handle part of the flamethrower around in the direction of the ant.

Simms squeezed the trigger on the flamethrower and a burst of flame went down the tunnel. There was a staggering rush of hot air back into Simms' face. He turned his face away. He felt sand dumping down on him as Cramer scrambled up the rope.

Simms fired off another blast at the ant. It kept the ant back, but he was going to cook himself if he kept this up in such close quarters. In addition, he could tell that the ant was keeping back far enough to not get burned by the flame. This situation would only last until the flamethrower ran out of fuel.

"OK, climb up." Regan yelled down to Simms.

Simms shook his head. "I'll never be able to climb fast enough."

"Damn." Regan said emphatically.

Simms fired off another blast of flame and yelled something.

"What happened?" Regan asked.

"I think I burned off my eyebrows." Simms said.

"Hey," Regan said, "I just thought of something. Tie the rope around yourself."

"Ah, yeah. That might work." Simms said. He fired a quick burst to buy himself a couple of minutes and grabbed the rope. He whipped it around his waist and made a couple of quick knots.

"OK." Simms yelled up the hole. He grabbed the flamethrower. The rope went tight and then painfully yanked Simms off his feet and slowly up the side of the hole. Simms watched below. Sure enough the ant's head suddenly popped out of the tunnel and turned upwards towards him. He shot flame down the hole, nearly setting his pants on fire. The ant backed down into the tunnel and after another couple of painful jerks Simms slid up over the edge of the hole.

"Wow, you do look toasted." Regan said looking at Simms with a smile.

Simms was about to say something when off in the distance was a bright flash and a faint explosive sound.

"What was that?" Cramer asked.

"Phosphorus." Simms said. "They're using it to keep the ants in the hole while they get ready to drop the gas. They started. We need to get this closed up."

Cramer jumped up and started spooling the line out as he hustled back towards the helicopter. Simms and Regan joined him. By the time they got to the helicopter the ant that was pursuing Simms was climbing out of the hole.

"Hit it." Simms said to Cramer.

Cramer jammed the detonator down and the area rocked with a boom. A huge dust cloud covered the area. It took a few minutes for the dust to drift away and just as it did there was a gentle thumping sound all around the three of them.

"Ow, shit." Regan sat ducking his head down. He bent over and picked something up from the ground.

"What is it?" Simms asked.

Regan stared at the thing he had picked up. He showed it to the other two. "I think it's a piece of an ant."

They looked around and saw small black pieces of ant steadily raining down.

"Guess we got that one." Cramer said.

"No shit." Regan agreed.

They checked that the hole was sealed and climbed back into the helicopter and up into the sky.

7

"Ah, there you guys are." General O'Brien said as Simms and Regan walked into the State Police station.

"Yes sir." Simms said. "We were held up trying to get back to the base. So were the ants all killed by the cyanide gas?"

O'Brien gave a tentative nod. "Well, yes, those ants were eliminated."

"Excellent." Regan said glancing over at Simms. "It's probably a little late for us to catch a flight back to Washington tonight."

"Uh, hate to break this to you guys, but we have another problem." O'Brien said.

"Oh?" Simms said.

"Yeah. According to Dr. Medford there were two new queen ants in that colony that escaped before we gassed it." O'Brien was clearly frustrated.

"Escaped? To where?" Simms asked.

O'Brien shook his head and sighed. "God knows. I have ordered flights from the air base to start patrolling."

"Patrolling where?" Simms asked.

"Apparently everywhere. Dr. Medford has no idea how far these damned ants can fly." O'Brien said.

"And no idea of what direction they might head?" Simms asked, already knowing the answer.

"No." O'Brien's voice held a certain resignation. "Dr. Medford thinks that if we can't track them down...well, they'll start new colonies and we might not find them until, well, until it's too late."

"Too late? Too late for what?" Regan asked.

"For us." O'Brien said.

"But it's just two ants, right?" Regan asked.

"Yeah, but those two ants will start laying eggs by the thousands and new queens which will fly off and create more colonies. They'll be popping up everywhere. They'll grow faster than we can eliminate them." O'Brien said shaking his head slowly.

"Holy shit." Regan said.

Simms sighed. "OK. What can we do?"

"Frankly, I don't know. I am off to Washington to brief the Joint Chiefs—-and your boss. We're going to need to come up with some kind of plan. In addition, I think we're going to need a hell of a lot of luck." O'Brien replied.

"Well, I think the only thing we can do right now is help, as best we can, in searching for these flying ants. Stopping them before they can create any new colonies or queens sounds like priority number one." Simms said.

O'Brien nodded. "I agree. I will make sure before I leave you have anything you need."

"Thank you, General." Simms said.

"Good luck." O'Brien said.

"To you too. I'm not sure which one of us has the tougher task. Facing the ants or the Joint Chiefs." Regan said smiling.

O'Brien gave a short laugh. "You may be right about that."

Early the following morning Simms and Regan found themselves in a plane flying west. They had a general area they were going to search, but it would be crazy luck if they found either of the queen ants. It was kind of like when they were hunting down the holes into the colony except the area to search this time was massive and they were trying to spot a moving target. They harbored no illusions about their chances of success.

Just deciding how high to fly was difficult. If they flew high up they could cover a larger area, but it meant that an ant that may have landed would be nearly impossible to spot since it wouldn't stand out significantly from the rocks, scraggly brush and cactus that dotted the landscape.

If they flew low they could clearly see an ant moving along on the ground or even a new colony hole, now that they were getting good at that, but if the queens were still airborne flying low made it extremely hard to see much of the surrounding air space.

If they flew somewhere in the middle they couldn't see the ground or the sky real well. In the end, they decided to fly at an altitude that was somewhere in the middle and hope for the best.

Regan yawned. They had been at this for a while. "There's nothing out here. Why can't we just spray the whole southwest with bug killer?"

"That might get the ants, if they're still in the southwest. And, based on the westerly winds, it would definitely get everyone east of the Mississippi eventually." Simms answered. He knew Regan wasn't being serious, but boredom was starting to get to him too.

Simms leaned forward to the pilot. "What's our plan for refueling?"

"We can land in Springerville and refuel. It's just into Arizona." The pilot replied.

"That sounds fine. Then we can—-" It was all Simms got out before something struck the small plane. Whatever it was it seemed to hit somewhere back towards the tail. It sent the plane into a couple of wild twists before the pilot got it back under control.

"What the hell was that?" Regan said looking all around them.

"I don't—-" Simms started again, but couldn't finish.

"Shit!" The pilot was saying as the plane dove down and to the left.

"Did you see what hit us that time?" Regan called up to the pilot.

"Didn't hit us." The pilot answered. "That was me. Something nearly took our nose off."

"Did you get a look at it?" Simms asked.

"No. Just a black blur." The pilot answered.

"A black blur?" Simms asked.

"There!" Regan said pointing out the right side of the plane.

Simms strained to look around Regan. Sure enough, a short distance off to their right. A flying black ant.

"Holy shit." Regan said. "What are the odds of that?"

"Amazing." Simms agreed.

They watched as the ant seem to circle in a steady downward direction. After another minute it was clearly going down to land.

"Can you get us down there?" Simms asked the pilot.

The pilot scanned the terrain below. He nodded. "Yeah. I think so. Looks pretty flat."

It took the pilot one abortive attempt before successfully making a rough landing on the desert sand. They climbed out and scanned the horizon.

"I think it's in that direction." Simms said and took a couple of steps in that direction before he felt Regan's hand on his sleeve.

"And...what exactly are we going to do when we catch up with it?" Regan asked. He held up his .45.

Simms hesitated. "Hmm, I see your point. Didn't really plan on a close encounter."

"Damn." The pilot was staring at the plane.

Simms and Regan turned around.

"What?" Simms asked.

The pilot pointed at the underside of the plane. "Cracked a strut on the landing gear."

"Well, you can get that fixed back at the air base, right?" Regan asked.

The pilot nodded. "Sure. But I can't take off with it like that."

"Damn. That's not good." Simms said.

"Ah, shit. It gets better." Regan said looking back over Simms' shoulder.

"What do you mean?" Simms asked.

Regan pointed and Simms turned around.

"You were right about where the ant was, but we don't need to go to it. It's coming for us." Regan said.

Simms covered his eyes to block out some of the sun. There was clearly a black thing moving quickly in their direction. Simms turned back and stared at the plane for a moment.

"Well, we can't stay here. That plane won't protect us. That ant would crush that easily." Simms said.

"What about those rocks over there?" Regan pointed. There was a small rock formation a short distance away.

Simms gave a quick shrug. "I guess. It beats standing here."

Simms, Regan and the pilot started jogging towards the rocks. After a short distance Regan glanced behind them.

"Uh, I think that ant is moving a hell of a lot faster than we are." Regan said.

Simms looked back. "Hmm, we may want to run, like, really fast now."

All three started sprinting as fast as they could manage in the soft and sandy soil. A look back at the progress of the ant told them that is was going to be close to see if they reached the rocks before the ant caught up with them.

Simms studied the rocks as they approached them trying to determine what they could use, if anything, to hide behind or under. They needed something big enough for the three of them and too small for a giant ant. That had to be the first time anyone ever had to consider that situation before, Simms thought.

They were getting close now and, at the last moment, Simms spotted what he was looking for. He grabbed Regan's arm. "This way."

Regan slapped the pilot's shoulder and all three veered left into a cleft in the rock formation. It went back about ten feet. The first three feet of it were wide enough for the ant to fit its head in, but it started narrowing quickly as they slid further into it.

Simms was the furthest in and pushed himself back as far as he possibly could. It was so tight he wasn't able to take a deep breath. The pilot was next. He was clearly panicked at the sight of the ant, now at the opening of the crevice. Regan was the furthest out.

The ant tried to lunge in and grab Regan, but it's head got wedged on either side by the rock walls of the crevice. It yanked its head back and tried the same thing twice more before finally determining that wasn't going to work. It studied the crevice for a moment before turning its head sideways and sliding deeper into the crevice. This time its pincers could almost brush the front of Regan's jacket.

"Damn." Regan said. "If it hooks me with one of those things I'll be in its teeth in a heartbeat."

"It doesn't have teeth." Simms gasped out. "Those are mandibles."

"Thanks." Regan said over his shoulder. "It's good to know the technical name for what's going to chew me into little pieces."

The ant was trying to force his head in a little further with each thrust. With the last attempt it's pincer had scratched at the front of Regan's jacket. Regan exhaled and tried to squish further back, but there was no more room. He braced himself.

The ant leaned back for another attempt. It seemed to hesitate. Then it moved a little further back from the crevice. Regan couldn't see it clearly. The wall of the crevice blocked his view. He could just see a part of the black head of the ant.

Nothing happened.

"What's happening?" Simms asked.

"Not sure." Regan said. "I can't see it very well. But feel free to climb over me and have a look for yourself."

"Take a look." Simms said. "I'm going to need to breathe soon."

Regan eased forward. He could see a little more of the ant. It didn't seem to be moving. He moved out to the edge of the crevice, fully prepared to dive backwards if necessary. He could here both the pilot and Simms sigh loudly.

"It's not moving." Regan said.

Simms joined Regan at the front of the crevice. The pilot hovered back in the more narrow part of the crevice.

"Definitely not moving." Simms said walking out and skirting around the ant. He had his .45 out and ready, though he knew it really wouldn't stop the ant if it came at him.

"Is it dead?" Regan asked.

"Well, I doubt it just fell asleep." Simms commented.

"So, we got one of the queens." Regan said.

Simms stood staring at the ant and thinking. "I don't think so."

"They said that the queens flew off. And it's got wings." Regan said pointing at the back of the ant. He no more than said it when one of the wings fell off. It slid down on to the sand.

"Not very good wings, I guess, but wings nonetheless." Regan added.

"I think this is one of the male ants. Dr. Medford said they accompanied the queens and after mating died. I think this is one of them." Simms said circling back around to where Regan was.

"So, we were just going to be his last meal." Regan said.

"Looks that way." Simms agreed. He turned back towards the pilot. "You said the plane can't take off."

The pilot had edged slowly out of the crevice to join them. He shook his head staring at the ant. "No. Can't take off."

"Does the radio still work?" Simms asked.

The pilot nodded, still staring at the ant. "Yeah. Are you sure it's dead?"

Simms nodded. "It's dead. Go call in. Have them send someone out to pick us up."

The pilot just stood there.

"Maybe it would be a good idea to get someone out here before another ant shows up." Simms said.

That woke the pilot up. He glanced at Simms with a certain lightly veiled terror in his eyes. He took off at a run towards the plane.

"You think another ant might be around here?" Regan asked.

Simms shook his head. "I doubt it. I just don't want to spend all night out here waiting for him to get his courage up enough to go to the plane and make the damned call."

8

"I know that look." Regan said as Simms finished his phone call with General O'Brien. "Something is up."

Simms walked over to the desk in the New Mexico State Police Station and sat on the corner. "They found the queens."

"Ah, good news for a change. I assume they killed them." Regan said.

"One of them." Simms said.

"Just one?" Regan asked hoping DCI Simms would change his answer.

"Just one. It landed on a ship at sea. Started making a nest in the hold. It killed most of the crew before the Navy could get there and sink the ship. One down." Simms explained.

"But you said they had found both?" Regan asked.

Simms nodded. "They're pretty sure the other one has taken up residence in the underground waterways beneath Los Angeles."

"Los Angeles? That can't be good." Regan said.

"Yeah. The Army is deploying there now. They're going to have to hunt them down in the tunnels on foot." Simms said.

Regan thought for a moment. "Oh, yeah. Guess you can't gas them out of there without gassing the whole city. Well, that's going to be an ugly job. Trying to get them out of there."

Simms didn't say anything.

Regan glanced up at Simms. "Oh, crap. We're heading to Los Angeles, aren't we?"

Simms nodded. "It's what we do."

Regan sighed as he stood up. "Yeah, but why do we always have to be the ones out front?"

Simms smiled. "Face it, you'd be bored if you weren't right in the middle of it all."

"I'm not opposed to being bored occasionally." Regan said.

"Come on." Simms said standing up. "General O'Brien has a jet waiting for us at the air base."

By the time Simms and Regan made it to Los Angeles evening was falling. They were driven into the city and down into the wide concrete aqua duct where the Army had set up a command post. It was at one of the entrances to the miles and miles of tunnels running under the city.

"Ah, glad you guys could make it in time. We're assigning different groups to move into the tunnels from all directions." Major Kibbee told Simms and Regan as they climbed out of a jeep and walked over to him.

"Where in the tunnels are the ants?" Simms asked.

Kibbee shrugged. "We don't know yet. We're going to have to just push on in until we encounter them. Once we do, we can concentrate our forces there."

"What can we do?" Simms asked.

Kibbee smiled. "I was hoping you would ask that."

"I really wasn't, but I knew he would." Regan said.

Kibbee laughed. "Well, I was thinking you could take charge of the group coming in from the North."

Simms nodded. "We can do that."

"How about it? You up for some more bug hunting?" Kibbee asked slapping Regan on the shoulder.

"Why not." Regan said. "The ants and I are getting to be old friends by now."

"Great. Let's take a look at the maps so I can brief you on the plan." Kibbee directed them over towards a table covered in maps.

They spent the next half hour going over the where Simms, Regan and the soldiers that would accompany them would go in at and the procedure to follow if they came across the ants. All units were carrying radios and were to report any contact with the ants. The other units could then converge on their location until the queen's chamber was located.

Dr. Medford had been very insistent upon that one point: they had to find the queen's chamber. It was only there they would be able to determine if any new queens had been born and if they had escaped this nest.

It took Simms and Regan and their army escort of two soldiers armed with flamethrowers almost an hour to reach the North tunnel entrance. It was wide enough at this point for them to be able to drive their jeep into the tunnel. From the map they carried it looked like they would be able to drive about a half mile before the tunnel narrowed and they would be forced to proceed on foot.

"I would feel better if this tunnel were big enough to allow a tank to drive in here." Regan commented.

"Can't see much from inside a tank." Simms said as he steered the jeep slowly around a corner.

"Can't get eaten by a giant ant from inside a tank either." Regan replied.

"Wait. Stop." Regan said putting a hand on Simms' arm.

Simms stopped the jeep. After a moment he turned the engine off. In the quiet of the tunnel there sounded the dying echo of the ant chirping noise they had heard in the desert. Simms and Regan looked around trying to gauge from which direction the sound had come, but the sound had faded away.

"Well?" Regan asked.

"Not sure. I guess we'll just keep going in this same direction. That looks to be the general direction that everyone else will be heading towards." Simms said with a shrug.

"Guess that's as good as any." Regan agreed.

Simms started the jeep back up and drove on. They had made two more turns always checking the map to see if they were headed in the right direction. Some intersections were easy to figure out because the alternative choice led to a dead end only a short distance in.

They finally reached an intersection where going forward or to the right, the only other option, with the jeep was impossible. The tunnel narrowed so that it was barely wide enough for two men to walk side by side. They climbed out of the jeep.

"Make sure you have those things ready." Simms said to the two soldiers as they climbed out of the jeep and readjusted the flamethrowers on their backs.

"Yes sir." They both answered.

Regan was leaning over the map which he had laid on the hood of the jeep. "Based on this...I'm thinking straight ahead." He pointed past the front of the jeep.

"That would have been my guess too." Simms agreed. Simms stepped in front of the jeep and started walking into the narrower tunnel.

"Hey, Elliot?" Regan asked.

Simms turned around. "Yeah?"

"I don't think you should go first." Regan said.

"Well, I appreciate your concern for my welfare, but it's OK. I'm alright going first." Simms said.

"Well, that's good, but not exactly what I was thinking. If we do encounter an ant and, well, one of these guys gets a little excited, you know, I...don't think you want to be in front of him." Regan waved towards the flamethrower.

"Hey, what are you sayin'?" One of the soldiers asked.

Regan turned to look the guy straight in the eye. "I'm saying, Private, that if you get trigger happy you could fry the shit out of someone with that thing."

"I've practiced with this weapon many times." The soldier replied indignantly.

"Ever seen one of these ants up close before?" Regan asked.

The soldier hesitated. "No."

Regan nodded. "Now's your chance. Go in the front."

The soldier hesitated again. He glanced over at Simms.

Simms nodded. "He's right. You need to be in front. I'll be right behind you with this." Simms held up his machine gun. "I promise I won't panic and shoot you."

The soldier huffed and walked past Simms and into the tunnel. He moved slowly forward waving his flashlight around ahead of him. Simms followed, then Regan and then the second soldier whose primary task was to watch behind them.

"I am guessing the walkie-talkie is useless in here." Simms said over his shoulder.

Regan pulled the walkie-talkie around and tried calling the command center, but got nothing except static.

"That would be a good guess." Regan confirmed.

They walked down the tunnel at a slow pace for a while. Twice they stopped to listen and thought they heard the chirping sound of the ants, but no ants appeared. Finally they came to an intersection. The tunnel they were in dumped into a wider area where three other tunnels also met. They walked out into the middle.

"Let's take a look at the map again." Simms said pulling it out. Regan stepped up next to him with a flashlight and they took a couple of minutes to decide where they thought they were.

"So maybe that way?" Regan asked pointing towards the tunnel directly across from the one they had just emerged from.

Simms nodded. "If we are where we think we are, I would agree."

"Holy shit!" The soldier that had been up front was at the entrance to the tunnel they were planning to head down. He was shining the flashlight down it when, in the shadows, a black object started moving quickly towards him. He stumbled backwards.

Simms caught the soldier and kept him from falling down. "The flamethrower." Simms reminded the soldier.

The soldier ignited the fuel and fired into the tunnel. After a moment he shut it off. Everyone stared down the tunnel to see if he had killed it. Dark movement further down the tunnel told them the ant was still alive. The ant was still far enough back in the tunnel that the flame didn't seriously harm it.

At the sound of a scream they turned to see the soldier in the back had been grabbed by an ant that had emerged out of the right side tunnel. He was being crushed in the pincers of the ant and kicking wildly.

The front soldier fired up the flamethrower again and swung around towards the second ant. Regan had to drop flat to the ground and roll away to avoid being incinerated. The flames engulfed the second ant and the other soldier. After a moment both ant and man ceased moving.

"Careful!" Simms yelled at the soldier. "Watch where you're pointing that!"

"Y-Yes...sir." The soldier was very clearly shaking.

Turning Simms fired his machine gun at the tunnel where the first ant had appeared. It was almost out into the junction with them. At Simms' feet, still on the ground, Regan opened fire at another ant that was now coming out of the left side tunnel.

"They didn't make any sound." Regan said.

Simms fired another burst. "Seems like that would have been the courteous thing for them to do."

"Yeah. A little warning would be nice." Regan agreed.

"We need to get out of here." Simms said.

Regan got to his feet. "Yeah."

"Back the way we came." Simms pointed towards the tunnel they had come out of. He pulled the soldier, who had just shot flame into the tunnel in front of them, and pushed him back towards Regan. "Take him with you."

Regan and the soldier backed down and into the tunnel. Simms turned to drive an ant back that had come out of the left side tunnel, but the ant managed to get out into the junction. It cut off Simms from following Regan and the soldier down the tunnel they had originally come out of.

"Elliot!" Regan yelled past the ant. "Hang on, we'll—-"

"Go!" Simms waved at Regan. "I'll go this way." He pointed at the right side tunnel where the burnt ant and second soldier lay.

"But—-" Regan started to say.

"Go. I'll meet up with you that way somewhere. Go!" Simms fired at the ant and ducked into the right tunnel.

The ant in the junction turned and started following Regan and the soldier. With a burst of flame the soldier toasted the ant and the two of them backed down the tunnel.

"Is he going to catch up with us?" The soldier asked.

"I sure as hell hope so." Regan said and reluctantly headed on down the tunnel. "Let's go."

9

"I gotta stop for a minute." The soldier said, huffing and leaning forward.

"OK." Regan said. "But only for a minute. I think that ant is still following us."

"This tank weighs a ton." The soldier said still sucking air.

"Yeah. Sorry. Didn't think we'd have to run so much." Regan said.

They were silent for a minute. There was no sound of any ants, though, they now knew that the ants could move pretty quietly.

"What's your name?" Regan asked.

"Johnson. Private Michael Johnson." The soldier replied.

"Well, I'm Robbie Regan of the OSO." Regan said.

A moment passed.

"Sir?" Johnson asked.

"Yeah?" Regan said.

"What's an OSO?"

"Huh. Yeah. We get that a lot. We investigate...trouble." Regan answered.

"Like the FBI." Johnson said.

"Well, kind of, but we deal with the really weird stuff. You know, when the shit's really hitting the fan." Regan said.

"Oh." Johnson nodded. "Well, I guess this qualifies."

"Yeah. Stuff like this." Regan said with a nod.

"So, you see a lot of this kind of stuff?" Johnson asked.

Regan sighed. "Sadly, yeah. We do."

Another quiet moment.

"If you don't mind me saying so, sir, your job kinda sucks." Johnson said.

"Yeah, I figured that out a while ago." Regan replied.

"So, why do you do it?" Johnson asked.

Regan shrugged. "Someone's got to."

"Guess so." Johnson said. "So why were we running? Why don't I just torch the ant when it catches up with us?"

"We could, but I'm not sure how many more ants we may run into before we get our asses out of here and I'm afraid that tank is going to run out of fuel." Regan explained.

"Yeah. I suppose so, but you have a machine gun." Johnson said.

"Trust me, it takes a lot of bullets to take one of these ants down. It wouldn't take more than a couple of ants before I run out of ammo." Regan said. "Let's start walking."

With a wave of his hand Regan began moving further on down the tunnel. He really hoped he could remember the way back to where they had left the jeep.

"Sir?" Johnson said as they were walking.

"Yeah?"

"I...I killed Guzman." Johnson's voice wavered.

"Guzman?" Regan glanced over at Johnson.

"The other soldier." Johnson answered quietly.

"Oh." Regan thought for a moment. "No, you didn't."

"But I burned him." Johnson said. "He was still alive."

"Hey, I've seen what those ants can do to a person. Honestly, this Guzman was, well, there wasn't any hope for him. There wasn't any way we were going to be able to shoot past him and kill that ant before it crushed him. You saved him from probably being eaten alive by them." Regan said.

"They do that?" Johnson asked.

"Oh yeah. We saw bones discarded outside the entrance to some of their holes out in the desert." Regan replied.

"Wow." Johnson said.

They walked quietly down the tunnel for another minute.

"Sir?" Johnson asked.

"Yeah?" Regan said.

"I don't want to get eaten by one of those things." Johnson said.

"Well, I don't either so let's figure out how to get the hell out of here." Regan said.

They came to a Y in the tunnel.

"Hmm, I don't remember this." Regan said staring at the decision. "Right or left?"

Johnson was about to say something when the ant chirping sound came out of the tunnel on the right. At almost the same time the sound also came from behind them. When they turned to look behind them there was an ant moving quickly towards them.

"OK. Torch that one." Regan said pointing towards the ant that had come from behind them.

Johnson turned and launched a blast of flame at the approaching ant. When he stopped and looked the ant still moved a little. He let out another burst, but it was short.

"Damn." Johnson said. "I think I'm out."

"Come on." Regan said and moved into the left tunnel of the Y. "Dump that flamethrower."

Johnson shucked the tank off his back and moved to the left tunnel. Suddenly out of the right tunnel of the Y an ant lunged at Johnson. One of its pincers tore into Johnson's side. He yelled and stumbled to the ground. Regan swung around and fired almost point blank with the machine gun into the face of the ant. The ant staggered back and then slumped to the ground.

"Can you move?" Regan asked kneeling next to Johnson.

"I think so." Johnson said holding an arm up against his side.

Regan helped Johnson up. They moved at what Regan felt was a painfully slow pace. They rounded a corner. Behind them could be heard the sound of another ant. It was easily going to catch them very soon.

"I see a ladder." Johnson said. The flashlight in Regan's hand danced around as they moved. They sped up slightly to get to the ladder. A sinking feeling hit them as the drew close to the ladder.

"Not a ladder." Johnson said.

"A grate." Regan said.

The sound of the ant was closing on them now. Regan looked at the grate and then back to the approaching ant. For some reason he looked up and there it was. A vertical shaft directly above them with a wrought iron ladder and a small pinpoint of light.

"Up there." Regan pointed. "Can you climb?"

"If the other option is getting eaten by an ant, I can climb." Johnson said.

"Good. Here." Regan put his hands out to hoist Johnson up. Johnson winced as he stepped into Regan's hand, but didn't hesitate. He grabbed hold of the ladder and pulled himself up. By the sound he was making it was obvious he was in a lot of pain, but he moved surprisingly fast.

Regan heard a scraping sound and turned to see the ant getting close. He swung his machine gun around and opened fire. It was a short burst before the gun clicked softly. Empty.

Regan threw the gun at the ant and jumped up to the bottom rung of the ladder. He scrambled up as fast as he could. Just as his leg was about to be drawn into the vertical shaft the end of the ant's pincer hooked the bottom of his trouser leg. For a brief second the material held and Regan thought he would get pulled back down, but then the pant leg tore and Regan pulled himself completely into the shaft.

Regan looked down. The shaft was too narrow for the ant's head to fit into. First time I was glad the damned things were so big, Regan thought.

Light suddenly streamed down the shaft. Regan looked up to see Johnson shoving a manhole cover aside. Regan looked down and saw the tear in his pant leg.

"That's going on the expense report." Regan said as he climbed out.

10

Simms hadn't traveled far down the tunnel when the thought crossed his mind that without the map he could be wandering through the maze of tunnels for quite a while—-and in the company of ants. He walked for a short distance and stopped. He listened. He repeated this pattern constantly checking behind him for ants.

Simms checked his ammo. He had half a clip left. That wasn't going to hold off very many ants. He stopped and listened. This time he heard something. He took a moment in order to determine if, by chance, it could be the sound of humans, but the more he listened the less the sound had any human quality to it. He decided running was his best option.

As he sprinted down the tunnel he could see he was coming up on a T junction. He had to decide whether to go left or right. He chose right and skidded around the corner. He nearly slid right into the pincers of an ant. He swung the gun around and fired off a quick burst. Spinning back he launched himself out of the right tunnel and into the left.

He ran as fast as he could not knowing if the ant behind him was in pursuit or not. He thought it was prudent to assume that it was.

After what seemed like a long run Simms came to another T junction he stopped and listened. He heard something, but it seemed out of place. It sounded like crying. Like a small whimpering cry to his left. Turning left he ran down what ended up being only a short side tunnel that abruptly stop in a dead end.

The sound was coming from a pile of old dirty tarps in the corner. Simms walked slowly over and lifted the tarps. It was a small girl huddled under them. There was a strong odor emanating from the tarps. It took Simms a moment to realize the smell was diesel fuel.

"Are you OK?" Simms asked kneeling down.

"I'm afraid." The girl said.

"I understand." Simms said. "How did you get here?"

"I got lost." The girl said. She was light haired and wearing a dirty yellow dress. She had dirt smudges on her face and she smelled like the diesel from the tarps.

Simms glanced around. They were in a bad spot here. Nowhere to run. It was amazing the ants hadn't gotten this girl already. The odor of the tarps worked its way into his thoughts. The diesel smell. The ants probably didn't like it so they avoided it. While that probably had saved the girl up to this point, Simms doubted the ants would be deterred enough by it to prevent them from coming after both him and the girl. They needed to get out of here.

"Come with me." Simms said to the girl holding out his hand. "We'll find our way out of here together."

The girl hesitated. "The monsters. They'll get us."

"I'll keep them away from us." Simms held up his machine gun. "With this."

The girl looked at the gun and then slowly stood up. She brushed off her dress, which did nothing to eliminate the dirty smudges on it. She took Simms' hand and they headed back down towards the T junction.

When they got back to the T junction an ant was scuttling towards them from the direction Simms had originally come from. The girl screamed and Simms fired at the ant to slow it down. He couldn't afford to expend the bullets necessary to kill it. Simms pulled the girl behind him as he moved as quickly as he could down the right side of the T junction. He knew the ant would still be following them.

They turned a corner and then another. Finally another T junction was visible ahead, not only in the light of the flashlight, but there was the unmistakable glow of daylight coming from the right side.

Just as they reached the T junction Simms could hear the sound of scuffling ant footsteps coming from the left tunnel. To the right the tunnel angled upwards and daylight was visible, though there was something in that tunnel as well. With little choice Simms and the girl moved towards the light.

As they moved closer to the light they heard more than one ant approaching from behind. There were no ants in this tunnel, but a metal grate blocked the tunnel. Part of the grate was bent out some.

"Can you get through that?" Simms asked the girl pointing towards the bent part.

"I'll try." The girl said and squeezed herself into and through it.

"Good." Simms said as he put his shoulder against the grate and pushed. The grate moved a little, but not enough for him to get through it. He was about to push again when the girl screamed.

Simms spun around and saw an ant almost to him. He fired his machine gun until the clip was empty. He watched the ant for a moment twitch a little and then felt certain it was dead. The tunnel had narrowed somewhat here so the dead ant now blocked any other ants from getting through to him. He was about to congratulate himself on his luck when the dead ant began to slide backwards. It was puzzling since he was pretty sure he had killed it. Then it dawned on him. There was another ant behind the dead one dragging it away. Once the live ant was able to pull the dead back to the junction it would be able to get past it.

Simms turned back to the girl. "Go find help."

The girl was going to say something and then simply turned and ran up the tunnel to the street level.

Simms put his shoulder into the grate again. It seemed like the grate wanted to move, but every time he thought it was close to bending out some more he lost his footing on the cement floor of the tunnel and the grate remained the same.

Simms looked back down the tunnel. The dead ant was just about to the T junction. Time was running out. He looked at the machine gun. It was powerful weapon as a gun, but it was fairly useless as a club.

From behind him he heard footsteps. Turning he saw the girl and a man running down the tunnel.

"This girl says you need help." The man said.

"Yes. Pull on the grate while I push." Simms said.

"OK." The man grabbed hold of the grate and braced himself. He started pulling as Simms pushed. The grate groaned and bent some. They stopped and caught their breath.

"Hey." The man said pointing down the tunnel. "I think there's something down there."

"Pull." Simms said with a big push against the grate. The man pulled as well and the grate bent some more. It didn't seem to Simms like it was wide enough, but when he glanced up at the face of the man and saw his expression of terror Simms decided it would have to be wide enough. With a painful, bruising effort Simms forced his way through the gap in the grate and crawled through.

With a clang the ant hit the grate. The girl screamed and ran up the tunnel away from it. With an equally little girl type of scream, the man did the same. Simms lay on his back looking up at the ant only feet away on the other side of the grate.

"Not today." Simms said to the ant. He wasn't sure if the grate would hold the ant back, but it would hold it long enough for him to get back on his feet and start running up the tunnel. He decided to forgo the screaming part.

11

"Hey!" Simms turned at the sound. He had been standing at a street corner trying to get his bearings. He was trying to figure out where they had originally come into the tunnels. He had left the little girl in the care of the man that had helped him through the grate.

From a block away Regan was helping Johnson cross a street towards Simms. Simms met them half way.

"You made it." Regan said.

"It was a close one." Simms admitted.

"Us too." Regan agreed.

"We need to—-" Simms started to say when two jeeps drove around the corner and screeched to a stop next to them. A soldier jumped out.

"DCI Simms?" The soldier asked.

"That's me." Simms replied.

"Sergeant Willis, sir. Got orders from General O'Brien to find you. They couldn't get a hold of you on the walkie-talkie." Willis said.

"Oh, yeah. I think an ant has ours." Regan said with a shrug. "Knowing those bastards they are probably listening in on it."

"Really?" Willis asked.

"Never mind him. What news from the General?" Simms said.

"General O'Brien says they have located the nest in drain 267." Willis said.

"Where is that?" Simms asked.

Willis waved at one of the soldiers and he handed over a map. Willis laid it out on the hood of the jeep.

"Right about here. They're sending in troops from multiple directions." Willis said pointing at a spot on the map.

"Where is that in relation to us?" Simms said staring down at the map.

"We're right here." Willis slid his finger a little further north.

"OK. So let's head for the nearest entry point that troops are going in at." Simms said.

"Johnson here needs a medic so we need to send him back with one of the jeeps." Regan said.

"Right." Simms agreed. "Sergeant, maybe you and one of your men can accompany us and the others can head back to the command center with Johnson."

"Sure thing, sir." Willis said and turned to give the orders.

"Oh, and make sure we have four flamethrowers with us. That's about the only thing that takes those things down."

"Yes sir." Willis replied.

The two jeeps parted ways. Simms, Regan, Willis and another soldier headed down a side street and around a corner in the general direction of the nearest entry point to drain 267. They were half way down a block when just ahead some people came pouring out the door of a bar and into the street in a clear state of panic.

Willis stopped the jeep and all four men got out.

"What's going on?" Simms called out.

A woman waved back towards the bar. "There! In there!"

A man stopped long enough to point behind him and say, "A giant ant!"

Simms grabbed a flamethrower.

"No." Simms said as Regan started to grab another flamethrower. "You stay here."

"Why?" Regan asked.

"In case more appear from other buildings." Simms answered.

"Ah, got it. OK." Regan said.

Simms slid the tank on to his back and went up to the front door of the bar. He pushed the door open with his foot. The bar was dim inside and it took Simms' eyes a moment to adjust. He caught some movement towards the back of the bar. Moving in for a closer look he saw an ant wedging itself behind the bar in search of something.

Simms moved to his left to get a better angle to burn the ant. Out of the corner of his eye a noticed more movement. Just a few feet to his left he realized a section of the floor had been torn out and the head of another ant was emerging.

Simms turned and sent flames down into the hole. The ant staggered back and disappeared back down into what was presumably the basement of the building. The ant behind the bar and taken notice of Simms and turned around. It got within a few feet of Simms before a jet of flame stopped it. Even while burning the ant seemed to be struggling forward trying to get Simms. He gave it a second blast and it slumped to the floor, still burning.

Simms stepped over to the hole in the floor. Peering down he couldn't see anything moving. He would have liked to blast flame down into the hole for good measure, but he was afraid of setting the entire building on fire.

Simms walked back out of the building and over to the jeep.

"Looked like you were having fun." Regan said.

"Found a couple in there. They came up through the floor. That means they could be coming up into any of these buildings." Simms said.

"Damn. Like, anywhere in the city." Regan said.

"Exactly." Simms set the flamethrower back into the jeep. "You better get on the walkie-talkie and let the General know he's going to need to deploy some troops throughout the city to stop any ants that escape up into the buildings or streets."

"Right." Regan said, taking the walkie-talkie from Sgt. Willis.

While Regan relayed their warning to the General, Simms turned to Willis. "How much further until we get to the entrance to drain 267?"

Willis stared down the street for a moment. "About two blocks down that way and then right and then maybe three more blocks."

"OK. Good." Simms said.

"Sir?" Willis said.

"Yeah?" Simms looked at Willis' dark expression.

"Some of the men were saying if they don't get the queens from this nest we might never stop them." Willis said, his voice quiet.

Simms sighed. He had seen that look before in people's eyes when faced with something like this. "Sergeant Willis, I won't lie to you and I won't sugar coat things. This is a very serious threat to us. Everything we have ever known may be at risk, but I have been through this kind of thing before and every time we have found a way to overcome it. I think the reason we always prevail is that we never give up. We never lose faith in ourselves. So, we just need to focus on what's right in front of us. The next thing we need to deal with and trust in ourselves and each other."

Willis stared at the ground for a moment and then looked up at Simms. "Thank you, sir. I guess I just needed to be reminded of that."

"Sometimes, we all need to be reminded of it." Simms said and smiled at Willis.

"So, the General says they were just talking about the possibility of the ants moving up into the buildings when I called." Regan said walking over to Simms and Willis. "He is calling in more troops to blanket the city, checking any and all access to the tunnels."

"Good. Shall we get moving?" Simms said.

All four of them climbed into the jeep and Willis drove on down the street. They got to the corner they needed to turn at when Regan reached forward and pulled at Simms' shoulder.

"Up there." Regan pointed.

Willis stopped the jeep at the corner and they all looked up at a six story apartment building. There were some people hanging out several windows on the third floor. They were yelling something and waving.

Simms got out of the jeep and crossed the intersection to the building. The other three men followed him.

"What's going on?" Simms called up to them.

A woman yelled down to him. "Those creatures are trying to get us."

"OK. We'll be right there." Simms shouted to her. He gestured to Regan and the other soldier to go get the flamethrowers.

"They're on the stairs! We can't stop them!" A man yelled out the window.

"We're coming." Simms called up to the man, but the man had already ducked back in the window.

Regan and the soldier returned and all four slipped on the flamethrowers. They moved to the front door of the apartment building. Simms tried the door, but it was locked.

"Figures." Simms said.

"Here." Willis stepped forward and kicked the door in.

"That works." Regan said as they walked into the lobby.

They could hear screams from upstairs somewhere. To the left in the small lobby was a reception desk. Straight back was an elevator and next to the elevator a narrow hall ran towards the back of the building. To the right were stairs. There was a gaping hole in the floor in front of the elevator and another hole was visible in the wall part of the way down the hall to the back.

Simms moved to the bottom of the stairs and stopped. He could see on the first landing the abdomen of an ant.

"Look out!" Regan said stepping forward towards the hole in front of the elevator which was just behind Simms. An ant's head was emerging from the hole. Regan shot a burst of flame into the hole and the ant retreated.

"There!" Willis pointed down the hall. An ant was coming out of hole in the wall. He stepped past Regan and shot a blast of fire down the hall. The ant backed into the hole, but was still visible further in the hole, just waiting to come back out.

Simms was about to burn the ant on the landing, but thought better of it. He wasn't sure he could kill it very easily from the backside and if he lit the stairs on fire one of the exits for the people up there would be cut off.

"This is a bad spot. Let's see if we can get up the back stairs." Simms said moving towards the hallway.

"Hang on." Willis said firing a blast into the hole in the hallway to keep the ant there at bay.

The four of them slid past the hole in the hallway and reached the back stairs. Two ants were in the hallway behind them now. One from the hallway hole and one from the elevator hole.

"Should we torch them?" The soldier in the back called forward.

Simms leaned back stared down the hallway. He could see past the two ants at two more ants emerging from the holes.

"No. Too many. At this rate we'll run out of fuel. Just keep them back from us." Simms said.

They reached the first landing and turned, climbing up the second floor. On the second floor they glanced down the hallway. There were no people, but there was an ant that turned at the sound of them and started towards them. Simms gave it a shot of flame and motioned for the rest of them to keep going up the stairs. When the rest of them were up to the next landing Simms fired a quick burst to deter the ant again and followed them.

As they rounded the landing leading to the third floor a lamp flew past Regan's head. He ducked.

"Hey!" Regan glanced up at a man standing at the top of the stairs on the third floor.

"Sorry!" he man yelled down. "I thought you were one of them."

"No. I only have two legs." Regan replied. All four of them climbed to the third floor.

"Watch those stairs." Simms told the soldier.

"They're tryin' to get up the other stairs. We piled furniture up to stop 'em, but they're tearin' it down." The man said, clearly frightened.

"We need to move higher up. Tell the people to come to these stairs." Simms said to the man.

Simms turned to Regan. "You and Sergeant Willis go with him. Torch an ant if you need to in order to slow them down."

"Right." Regan said and the man led them down the hall.

Simms heard the whooshing sound of a flamethrower behind him. He turned to see the soldier burning the head of an ant trying to get up the stairs.

"You burn one and the one behind it doesn't care. It just keeps coming. They're not afraid of dying." The soldier said exasperated.

"Yeah. They're pretty single-minded." Simms said.

People started scurrying down the hallway towards Simms. As they came up to him he sent them on up the stairs. He stopped one man as he passed.

"Is everyone out of the apartments on the first two floors?" Simms asked the man.

"I think so. Everyone came out when the screaming started." The man said.

"OK. Make sure you get everyone out of their apartments as you people go up. Go all the way to the top. Can you access the roof?" Simms asked.

The man nodded. "Yeah. We can."

"Good. Go." Simms said.

"Are you with the army?" The man asked.

"No. The OSO." Simms replied.

The man started up the stairs and stopped. "Sir, what's an OSO?"

Simms waved him off. "Go."

At the end of the line of people Regan and Willis appeared.

"Those bastards are getting pretty aggressive." Regan said.

"Their colony is probably growing and I doubt there's much food in those tunnels." Simms replied.

"Well, I'm not on the menu." Regan said firmly.

They started up the stairs. There was a cry and Simms, Regan and Willis looked back to see the other soldier pulled down the stairs by the pincers of an ant. The soldier slid down the stairs underneath the first ant and into pincers of the second ant. It happened so fast the three of them could do nothing to save him. Willis turned a shower of fire down on to the first ant to drive it back.

They got to the next floor.

"So what's our plan. You realize that at some point up there we're going to run out of building, right?" Regan asked.

"Yeah, well, the plan is a work in progress right now." Simms said.

"Damn things." Willis said as he let loose a stream of flame at the ants pursuing them. "They're fast bastards."

When they reached the roof there was about thirty people nervously milling about.

"Is the army coming to kill those things?" A woman asked.

Simms nodded. "Yes, but...not before we are going to have to get off this roof."

The woman stared at Simms as he started circling around the edge of the roof.

"Here!" Simms called back to Regan and Willis. They joined him at the north edge of the roof.

Simms pointed down. "There's a fire escape here that goes down two stories to the neighboring roof. Sergeant Willis take the people down there and then make your way down to the street."

"Yes sir." Willis said moving up.

"Aren't we going too?" Regan asked.

"We will, but we have something to do first." Simms said walking back to the door to the stairs that led back down into the building.

"And what would that be?" Regan asked walking along.

"This building is probably full of ants by now. If this building were to be destroyed..." Simms said.

"You mean burn the building down? This is a big building." Regan pointed out.

"And that's a lot of ants." Simms countered.

"Alright, but if we burn the city down I'm telling everyone it was your idea." Regan said with a smile.

"Deal." Simms prepared his flamethrower and then started torching the door and the stairs. Regan added the flame from his flamethrower. They sprayed flame around the roof as they steadily backed towards fire escape steps.

When their tanks were empty they tossed them aside. As they stood at the top of the fire escape steps an ant emerged from the flaming door to the stairs. It was burning as it moved across the roof towards them. Amazed at the tenacity of the ant the two of them just stood watching it approach. Its speed slowed the closer it got to them. At about ten feet away the ant slumped down and stopped moving.

Simms and Regan looked at each other.

"Tough bastards." Regan said.

"They are." Simms agreed and the two of them climbed down the steps.

By the time they reached street level with all the residents of the apartment building there was fire visible down to the fifth floor.

"Better move these people further away." Simms said.

"Yeah. Not sure those ants won't come spilling out on to the street to avoid the fire." Regan said.

"My guess is they will go back down into the tunnels." Simms replied.

"They can keep right on going down straight to hell as far as I'm concerned." Regan said.

"Agreed." Simms said as they ushered the people further up the block.

12

Simms and Regan arrived back at the Command Center to find General O'Brien, Major Kibbee, Agent Graham and the Medfords gathered around a map. After a brief greeting they were told about the loss of Sergeant Peterson. He died saving two missing boys that were trapped by ants in the tunnels. There was good news, however, in that they were certain they had killed the queen ant and some newly hatched queen ants.

Simms and Regan related the events of what happened in the north section of tunnels—-including burning down a building.

"I understand your circumstances DCI Simms, but let's hope it doesn't come down to burning the whole city down to drive those damned things out of here. So, Dr. Medford, with the queens gone what will the rest of the colony do?" General O'Brien asked.

"Well, General, they will continue to forage for food. They will carry on their usual duties for a while despite not having a queen. They really don't know anything else to do." Dr. Medford explained.

"So we can expect them to continue to raid into buildings?" Regan asked.

"I'm afraid so." Dr. Medford replied.

"Well, I have more men coming in from Pendelton and we will utilize police and firemen to monitor every building for ants. It seems like we will have to hunt down and kill every last one of them." O'Brien said disgustedly.

"And what about the desert?" Simms asked.

"What about the desert?" O'Brien asked.

"Are we sure that was the only ant colony affected by the atomic testing in New Mexico?" Simms asked.

Everyone was silent for a moment.

"Damn." O'Brien said quietly.

"Dr. Medford, in your estimation, how many ant colonies could there be in, say, a 200 mile radius of Alamogordo?" Major Kibbee asked.

Dr. Medford looked gravely around the group. "My goodness. There could be thousands of colonies."

Again everyone was silent.

"So..." Agent Graham said slowly, "there could be thousands more of these giant ants out there? If that's true, well, we don't stand a chance. It was a major effort just getting rid of two small colonies."

"But there haven't been any more sightings." Regan pointed out.

"He's right. If there were more colonies we should have heard about more sightings." Pat Medford said.

"Maybe, just maybe, we have been very lucky." Dr. Medford said.

"What do you mean?" O'Brien asked.

"Well, perhaps what happened to these ants was the result of a unique set of circumstances." Dr. Medford answered.

"Like what?" Simms asked.

"Suppose for this mutation to occur the ants needed to be at just right distance away from an atomic blast and maybe even at just the right moment of the mating process for this to happen." Dr. Medford explained.

"Let's hope so." Simms said solemnly.

"Yeah, because we really don't have time to keep chasing these ants." Regan said.

"You got something bigger to be dealing with?" Graham asked.

"In our line of work, yeah, by next week there will be something bigger for us to deal with." Regan glanced over at Simms.

Simms nodded. "Does seem that way."

"Did anyone ever tell you your job sucks?" Major Kibbee asked with a smile.

Regan nodded. "Yeah, we get that a lot."

K McConnell

www.kmcconnellbooks.com[1]

kmcconnell@kmcconnellbooks.com

---

1.   http://www.kmcconnellbooks.com/

The Hamlet Mysteries series...
To Not Be In Hamlet

Sam MacNeil, part time mystery writer, has returned to his hometown to house sit for his parents as they start a lengthy vacation. What Sam has forgotten while away is the quirky weirdness of the little town of Hamlet. With expectations that he would quietly do his time in Hamlet the discovery of a dead body, clearly murdered, changes everything. Now Sam finds, much to his chagrin, the residents of Hamlet are expecting him to solve the murder. Not only does Sam not want to be involved in it, but the authroities have made it clear his help is not wanted. Was it the angry businessman from Detroit? Was it the shifty handyman the victim worked with? Sam doesn't know, but when killers from Detroit show up the situation is taking a serious and deadly turn. And then there's Becky. An old friend who clearly has more than friendship on her mind. Murder, killers and romance...this is not how this brief stay in Hamlet was supposed to go.

The Art of Hamlet

An old family friend asks Sam to look into a break in at her house. She is an art collector and critic, but nothing has been stolen and the only thing disturbed are some small statues. While it is a puzzling incident Sam doesn't think it is a serious issue, but when a neighbor is murdered and found bobbing in a nearby lake the story is once again taking a dark turn. As usual Sam is not inclined to get involved in a murder investigation, but somehow he seems to be sliding in that direction anyway. In addition, the County Detective seems to have recognized that Sam might be of some use—-regardless of the consequences for Sam. And what of Sam's old classmate, who is now a seemingly crazy hermit, ranting on about terrorists in Hamlet? Is that actually possible? To complicate things even further something is happening between Sam and Becky. Love and Death seem to be chasing Sam through the wacky streets of Hamlet.

Ophelia's Hunt

Sam's women troubles have seemingly tripled. There is Becky and the relationship that Sam has found himself in with her. However, suddenly, there is Callie. Sam's wealthy and wild ex-fiance who has appeared in Hamlet. Is she here to get Sam back? Everyone thinks so—-including Becky. Then there's the beautiful woman named Misty. She seems to have a particular interest in Sam as well. And, of course, there's murder in Hamlet once again. Questions abound. Is the lovely Misty a suspect or a new love interest? Who are the men stalking Callie? How is Sam going explain all of this to an increasingly angry Becky? Why is the County Detective actually soliciting Sam's help? Should Sam be flattered or very careful? With love and murder swirling around Sam how is he going to survive this?

The Ghosts of Hamlet

Sam MacNeil, part time writer, is house sitting for his parents in his hometown of Hamlet. The people of Hamlet are far more quirky than Sam remembers from his childhood and he is keen on leaving them behind and getting his life back, but it's those dead bodies that are the real problem. They just keep showing up. Murder in the small town of Hamlet has taken a noticeable uptick since Sam has returned and the residents have taken notice. Sam claims it has nothing to do with him and yet...Now, even worse, the residents are seeing ghosts and they blame Sam for that as well.

Sam may get his chance to escape Hamlet now that his parents are heading home, but can he really walk away without solving the mystery of the ghosts? Will he get away before the "gangsters" from Detroit catch up with him and turn him into a ghost? And what about Becky? He really wasn't planning on a romantic entanglement to muddle things up.

So what do ghosts, gangsters, girlfriends, musk ox and talking cans of beans all have in common? Sam MacNeil and the quirky town of Hamlet, of course.

The Play of Hamlet

It is finally here. The Founder's Day festival in Hamlet. A gala event highlighted by a play depicting the bizarre founding of Hamlet. Sam is not only the star of the play, but also a target for Scanlon and his killers from Detroit. They are determined to finish him off once and for all. But Sam knows they are coming and, with the help of the quirky residents of Hamlet, he has his own plans in the works. What Sam doesn't know is that Scanlon isn't the only killer from Sam's past that is out to get him. Could the biggest day of the year in Hamlet be Sam's last?

The King of Hamlet

The sixth story in the Hamlet Mystery series starts out where most of the stories end up...with a dead body. The trouble is Sam is found standing over the dead body and refusing to explain what has happened. He seems willing to take the fall for the guy's murder, but he is clearly hiding something. His friends are sure he didn't commit murder, but who is he protecting and why? What Sam is not telling anyone is that he is playing a more dangerous game than any of them can imagine. As bodies begin piling up around Sam he is increasingly wondering if he has a guardian angel or has become an unwilling accomplice to the Angel of Death. Once again women and murder are causing headaches for Sam.

The Graves of Hamlet

As if the town of Hamlet didn't have enough trouble with dead bodies now, it appears, someone is digging them up in the cemetary. The quirky residents of Hamlet are sure this has something to do with Sam. As usual Sam doesn't really want anything to do with whatever is going on, but when someone tries to make the cemetary Sam's premanent home one dark night it would seem that Sam will need to sort this out—-if only to save himself. To add to the confusion, with Becky out of town, Sam must also figure out who the half naked woman is that keeps showing up on his deck sun bathing. Oh, and who are these other guys that just showed up in Hamlet? The grandson of the recently deceased retired cop who is lying about his real identity and the suspicious looking guy casually asking questions around town about the same dead cop...?

Polonius' Plight

Here's a surprise...there's been a murder in Hamlet—-again. This time, however, Sam is very much intentionally involved. It's the suspects. The guy was found with a gaping shotgun blast to the chest. Like the one in the trunk of Renee's car. Of course the last person to be seen with the murder victim was Jen—-and she seems to have disappeared. And why is Reese, the County Detective looking for Becky and her grandfather's .38? Sam is sure none of his friends are murderers, but to keep any and all of them out of jail he needs to find out who the killer is and fast. To make matters worse, while Sam is trying to solve a murder and hide his friends the Town Council of Hamlet has had enough of Sam and the murders that seem to follow him around. They passed yet another of their many bizarre ordinances. Sam has been ordered to leave Hamlet.

The Office of Scientific Operations

With the conclusion of the traumatic events in 1933 surrounding the shocking affair involving the city of New York and a beast commonly referred to as "King Kong", the president of the United States, Franklin Roosevelt, established the Office of Scientific Operations (OSO). The purpose of the OSO was to monitor and evaluate the level of risk and assist in any manner the mitigation of danger of any and all scientific operations and anomalies. With the rapid pace of scientific discovery this office was given the highest priority and clearance to investigate any potential threats or consequences to the interests of the United States of America.

What follows are the real stories behind the cinematic cover-ups presented to the general public...

Release #2
from the declassified files of the
Office of Scientific Operations...

From 1954...

File #159 (commonly referred to by the public as "Terror in the Jungle")

OSO agent Jonathon Wyatt is pulled off vacation to an island in Indonesia to investigate sightings of pteranodons. The island is not far from the island known infamously as Z Land. It was once the headquarters of Dr. Zeitner whose experiments in genetically manipulating prehistoric monsters terrorized the world in the 1930s before the OSO put a stop to it. Wyatt's job is to determine if these are indeed Dr. Zeitner's creatures, but what he finds is much more deadly. This is no way to spend a vacation—-trying not to get eaten.

Release #3

from the declassified files of the

Office of Scientific Operations...

From 1954...

File #161 (commonly referred to by the public as "Revenge of the Creature")

After the capture of an unknown species of half man half fish is brought back to a Florida marine institute, OSO agents Wayne and Wyatt must determine the risk to the American people it poses. When the creature escapes and begins terrorizing the citizens of Florida the risk becomes all too real. Now they must hunt it down and stop it's killing spree, if they can.

From 1955...

File #165 (commonly referred to by the public as "It Came From Beneath the Sea")

OSO agents Simms and Regan are sent out to Pearl Harbor to investigate damage to one of the Navy's most advanced atomic submarines by some kind of giant creature. While the Navy has a hard time believing it, the OSO knows such creatures are real. It soon becomes apparent by the large number of ships being lost that something dangerous is hunting throughout the Pacific. Now, with the creature openly attacking the west coast of the United States Simms and Regan join the fight to stop this thing before the entire Pacific is destroyed by it.

Release #4

from the declassified files of the

Office of Scientific Operations...

From 1954...

File #163 (commonly referred to by the public as "The DC Creeper")

On a break from hunting monsters for the Office of Scientific Operations, OSO Agent Wyatt is trying to adjust to a more crowded domestic life. As brutally murdered bodies begin showing up in the nation's capitol, though, this doesn't seem like it is going to be much of a break. The newspapers have dubbed the hulking killer "The Creeper" and it looks like Wyatt is going to have to hunt him down and stop him before Wyatt becomes the next victim.

Release #5

from the declassified files of the

Office of Scientific Operations...

From 1956...

File #166 (commonly referred to by the public as "Tarantula")

Agents Simms and Regan from the Office of Scientific Operations, the OSO, returning from the Pacific Coast having just finished dealing with yet another monster threatening the United States are redirected to a small town in Arizona to verify that a large tarantula that has been terrorizing the local inhabitants has been destroyed by the Air Force. With Beka, a woman who insists on tagging along with the intrepid agents—-a clear violation of official regulations—-in tow, they quickly discover that the threat of the giant spiders in the Arizona desert are not over just yet.

From 1956...

File #171 (commonly referred to by the public as "Invasion of the Body Snatchers")

The Office of Scientific Operations, the OSO, has sent agents Wayne and Wyatt out to the small California city of Santa Mira to locate a missing Air Force major, sent to investigate the impact of some meteors, and to understand the meaning of his last cryptic message to Washington. What they find is that, while the city of Santa Mira may look like a quaint place to visit it soon becomes apparent that a missing Air Force major is the least of Wayne and Wyatt's problems. There is something very strange and deadly going on in Santa Mira. Something that seems...alien?

The New Sheriff

Travis Ames, somehow, has developed super powers. Exactly what these powers entail he's not sure. He's still learning how to control his powers, but he's already decided that he should use this new found power to fight crime. And...if he made a little profit along the way, well, that wouldn't be so bad either. But reality has a way of altering the best laid plans. He has quickly figured out he has no idea how to go about crime fighting. And, to make matters worse, he has learned the hard way, his new powers won't protect him from getting hurt or, quite possibly, killed. Can he survive long enough to learn how to use his powers? Can he get an aging detective to teach him how to fight crime? Can he prevent Aubrey, the new girl, and everyone else at work from figuring out what he can do? How long can he keep this up before he makes that one small mistake and ends up dead?

Don't miss out!

Visit the website below and you can sign up to receive emails whenever K McConnell publishes a new book. There's no charge and no obligation.

https://books2read.com/r/B-A-CGLDB-SWQVC

BOOKS 2 READ

Connecting independent readers to independent writers.

Also by K McConnell

Office of Scientific Operations
Office of Scientific Operations - Release #1

The Hamlet Mysteries
The Hamlet Mysteries 1
The Hamlet Mysteries 3

Standalone
A Conspiracy in Blood
Symbiotic Puppets
The Plague
The Club of the Bombastic Few
The Master Switch
Hamlet On A Budget
The New Sheriff
Office of Scientific Operations - Declassified Files (Release #2)
Office of Scientific Operations Release #3
Office of Scientific Operations - Declassified Files (Release #4)
Office of Scientific Operations - Declassified Files (Release #5)
The Hamlet Mysteries 2

Office of Scientific Operations - Release #6
The Hamlet Mysteries 1 - 9
The Trench of the Dead
The Heart of a Monster

Watch for more at www.kmcconnellbooks.com.

www.ingramcontent.com/pod-product-compliance
Lightning Source LLC
Chambersburg PA
CBHW051833130726
47987CB00002B/521

9 798230 207368